PROLOGUE

The monstrous cannon belched fiery spheres of death from their gaping maws with a deafening roar of thunder and a great cloud of blinding smoke. Their cannonballs screamed through the air, temporarily illuminating the predawn sky and then crashing into the Alamo's walls, sending shards of mortar flying twenty feet in all directions. Dimly, through the clouds of smoke, I could see the pinpoint pricks of light that were rifles firing and hear the screams and yells of men caught up in the deadly madness of battle.

"Sam," Danny yelled, "I need that rifle now!"

It seemed as though I was moving in slow motion as my hands shook and my heart pounded wildly. I tried to concentrate on loading his spare rifle. Powder...ball in patch...ram it home... powder in firing pan. I threw the rifle to him and grabbed the one he had just fired. I briefly peered over the palisade wall and saw hundreds of Mexican soldiers running to breach this little pile of logs that we were trying to defend. Powder...ball in patch...ram it home...powder in the firing pan...hand the rifle to Danny.

Suddenly, above the din of the battle, I heard Gregorio Esparza cry out, "Pared norte!"

I turned just in time to see Santa Anna's Army pouring over every wall of the Alamo using their makeshift ladders. Danny handed me a rifle. Powder…ball in patch…ram it home…powder in the firing pan.

Out of the corner of my eye, I could see the Alamo Chapel. Several Mexican soldiers entered the chapel, and then I heard rapid rifle and pistol fire and knew that they had found Colonel Bowie lying on his sickbed. To the right of us, I saw Uncle Micajah crumble under the enemy's fire, and Colonel Crockett valiantly clubbing the enemy with his rifle before finally succumbing to the overwhelming numbers of Mexican soldados.

"Samantha!" Danny demanded impatiently. Blinded by tears, I resumed loading his rifles. Powder…ball in patch…ram it home… powder in firing pan. Just then, my most feared, awful, unthinkable nightmare became reality. A Mexican soldier, looming out of the smoky darkness, his dark brown eyes glowing with hatred and the flames from the weapons firing around him, shot my Danny in the head and he fell back into my arms. Everything seemed to move in slow motion as I stared up at him in fear and horror. As I raised the rifle Danny had just given me to load to shoot the soldado, the back of my head exploded with pain, then everything went black.

GENERAL HOUSTON'S
LITTLE SPY

CARA SKINNER

GENERAL HOUSTON'S HOUSTON'S LITTLE SPY

A Texas Revolution Story

TATE PUBLISHING
AND ENTERPRISES, LLC

Published by Tate Publishing & Enterprises, LLC
127 E. Trade Center Terrace | Mustang, Oklahoma 73064 USA
1.888.361.9473 | www.tatepublishing.com

Tate Publishing is committed to excellence in the publishing industry. The company reflects the philosophy established by the founders, based on Psalm 68:11,
"The Lord gave the word and great was the company of those who published it."

Book design copyright © 2015 by Tate Publishing, LLC. All rights reserved.
Cover design by Rtor Maghuyop
Interior design by Jomar Ouano

Published in the United States of America

ISBN: 978-1-68028-436-2
1. Fiction / Historical
2. Fiction / Romance / Historical / General
15.06.03

Thanks so much to my friends Theresa Havel and Donna Davis for their encouragement and assistance in editing my work; my cousin, Lynn Spain for his knowledge of rifles used during this period; my husband, Larry Skinner, for his suggestions and support during the writing of this book; and my parents and grandmother who encouraged my love of Texas history.

1

My name is Samantha Russell and I will never forget the day the Alamo fell. I had been spared the horrible death that had befallen the men who fought in the Alamo, but, at that moment, I wished I had died with them. As I sat hidden in a copse of trees on the east side of town, I could see bright red flames lick the sky from the pyres built to burn the Texian dead illuminating the whole town in a pale, orange glow. The acrid smell of smoke drifted toward me as a cold, north wind blew over the land, causing me to shiver uncontrollably in the damp night air. Danny's body was on one of those pyres, and with that thought, my throat constricted and tears flooded my eyes. I just wanted to lie forever under those trees and sink into dark oblivion. I closed my eyes and let my mind drift to thoughts of home.

I was born on November 21, 1819, on my family's small farm near the Nolichucky River in eastern Tennessee. We owned about seventy acres of very rich river bottom land on which we raised twenty head of cattle, two horses, a mule, a pig or two, and plenty of chickens. We raised corn and wheat which we grew for our own consumption, to feed the livestock, and to sell. Ma raised a vegetable garden for the family, and we also had a small orchard with three apple and three peach trees. Pa and my brother, Luke, loved to hunt so we were invariably eating some poor wild creature.

My parents were Joseph and Sarah Russell and they had five children: Elizabeth, Luke, me, Ben, and Becky. Being the middle child had its drawbacks and its advantages. The obvious major drawback was the fact that I, being in the middle, was pretty much ignored unless I had gotten into trouble or there was work to do. Of course, this also proved to be the major advantage since, unless either of those two things occurred, I was left to my own devices and free to do as I pleased.

Elizabeth, who was four years older than me, was prissy and very dramatic. The only things she cared about were boys and how she looked. I have to admit, Elizabeth was very pretty. She had inherited Ma's blond hair, blue eyes, and perfect complexion, and from the time she turned sixteen, commanded every young man's attention at church and social events. She loved all the attention, but I could tell that Ma and Pa did not. Elizabeth and I didn't get along very well, mainly because she and I were not interested in the same things. I was more of a tomboy and really couldn't have cared less about pretty dresses or parties. The thing that irritated me most about Elizabeth was that she pouted and whined whenever she didn't get her way, and Pa and Ma let her get away with it.

I got along pretty well with Luke. He was three years older than me and looked more like Pa with his brownish-red hair and green eyes. He ignored me most of the time, but sometimes, when he was not helping Pa, tending the cattle, or visiting his girlfriend Rachel Collins, he would take me hunting and let me shoot his rifle. Of course, he had to prop the large rifle up on a rock or stump and I would just shoot at a tree. For someone so scatterbrained and obsessed with the opposite sex, he could be really patient with me. He even bragged that I was a pretty good shot…for a skinny little girl. Then he would whack the back of my head and I would hit him in the arm and we would fight all the way back to the house.

Ben and Becky were a lot younger than the rest of us and also had Ma's hair and eyes. In time they would grow up to be very intelligent, respectable people, but at the time, they were just small, snotty-nosed nuisances. I tried to entertain them as much as possible to give Ma some peace. I guess that's why they were constantly clinging to me, which really irritated me sometimes because all I wanted to do was go places with my best friend, Danny Autry.

Danny's family lived on a farm about five miles south of our place. He was two years older than me and had two older sisters and one older brother. I always had the impression that Danny's entry into the world was kind of an unexpected surprise to his parents because there was a five-year gap between him and the next-to-the-youngest sibling. Anyway, I didn't really know his sisters and brother, and so I didn't really care. All I cared about was Danny. We first met when I was three years old and he was five. His family came over to welcome us to the community after we moved into our new cabin, and the first thing Danny did was knock me down while running around playing with our dog, Blackie. Needless to say, our relationship continued to be a pretty rough and tumble one.

Danny and Luke never really got along because Luke always wanted to be around kids older than him, and then he fell in love (ugh) with Rachel Collins, so Danny was stuck playing with me. He didn't seem to mind though, and as for me, I worshipped the very ground on which he walked. Danny taught me how to fish and shoot a slingshot. I was really good at it too! I could hit squirrels and rabbits right between the eyes. We would kill a mess of squirrels or five or six rabbits, dress them, and bring them home for supper. My mother was just thrilled of course. She so wanted me to act as a young lady should, but I just couldn't do it.

Ten other families owned farms near ours. All the families decided we should form a community and provide schooling and church services for the families living there. The men chose a piece of land that was centrally located and erected a building that served as both a school and a church. The building consisted of two rooms: the smaller room was used for the school and contained desks and a large slate board on which Mrs. Gerrard wrote our lessons. The larger room was the sanctuary for the church. I always thought it was such a beautiful room. The pews and altar were hand carved by Mr. Gerrard. The pews were decorated with ornately carved backs, and the front of the altar was engraved with three beautiful crosses which matched the breathtakingly beautiful stained glass window featuring Christ's cross that adorned the front wall of the sanctuary. Mr. Gerrard had had that window especially created for our church at his own expense, and it was most definitely the pride of our community.

Mr. Gerrard served as our pastor and his wife, Rachel, taught school. Mrs. Gerrard taught reading, writing, mathematics, history, and science, and I never ceased to be amazed by the extent of her knowledge of all of these subjects. She was a great teacher and I loved attending her classes. The Gerrards, it turned out, were related to a very prominent Tennessee family. Mr. Gerrard's second cousin, David Gerrard, helped found the town of Gerrardstown, Virginia.

I loved school, especially reading, and Mrs. Gerrard kind of took me under her wing. She would loan me books from her massive private collection. I would spend hours down by the river fighting epic battles in ancient Greece as I read *The Iliad* and *The Odyssey* and crying over the tragedies of Shakespeare. I also really enjoyed science because our science class was held outdoors during good-weather days so that we could study animals and plants in their natural environment. Although math was not my favorite subject, I had inherited a natural aptitude for it from Pa and could add, subtract, multiply, and divide numbers mentally.

Because I enjoyed school so much, I remember Mrs. Gerrard saying, "Samantha, you have a very inquisitive mind and a love of adventure and learning. Promise me you won't let either one dim with age."

"Yes, ma'am," I promised, though I wasn't exactly sure what she meant until many years later. Danny was a good student also. So since our performance in school pleased our parents, we were subjected to less parental nagging and more free time to spend together.

What did not please our parents were our actions on Sunday. We both enjoyed Sunday school but just could not sit through two hours of Pastor Gerrard's sermons. He would drone on and on and on about hellfire and salvation, which always managed to put me to sleep. Before I knew it, my head would be nodding and then resting on the back of the bench with my mouth open, quietly snoring and drool running down the front of my dress. My mother would pinch me under the arm, which would jerk me awake in a most annoying and unpleasant way, but no matter how hard I tried to stay awake, it wasn't long before I was back to snoring and drooling.

Danny and I discussed the situation at length and agreed that we should skip out after Sunday school. Ma was so busy corralling my little brother and sister, and Pa was so busy talking farming and politics, that they never noticed. Danny and I would go down to the river and pick blackberries in the spring or grapes in the summer. Sometimes we would just sit on the bank and watch the sun glinting on the river's rapidly flowing current as it bounced off of rocks and raced downstream. In the winter, we would trudge through the snow along the bank or see how far we could walk out on the frozen river without slipping down on the ice. Now that I'm thinking back, it's a wonder we didn't fall through the ice and freeze to death. I guess the Good Lord didn't disapprove of us skipping services, or else he really does watch out for "fools and little children." Since we probably fell into both categories, we were most likely doubly protected. Anyway for me, Sundays were the best!

Ahhh…life was perfect. It was perfect—that is, until the year I turned fourteen.

2

I turned fourteen on November 21, 1833. Actually, since my birthday came right at the end of harvest time, it usually was forgotten until Ma placed the birthday cake she had made me on the table for dessert after dinner. Everyone was usually too busy preparing for another long, cold Tennessee winter to remember. Pa and Luke would butcher and smoke a hog, which, along with the calf we would butcher, provided us with plenty of meat for the winter. They would either store the meat in barrels covered with brine water or make it into jerky. Ma, Elizabeth, and I would finish gathering vegetables and fruit from the vegetable garden and orchard. Then we would pickle vegetables and put up fruit for weeks—at least it seemed that way. Preparing for the winter was a long, tedious task. The fact that my birthday was never a big family affair never really bothered me; first of all because I was too busy working, and second because…well, I was just another year older.

Harvest time was always one of my favorite times of the year because it provided numerous opportunities for social gatherings. All the men in the community would come together and help each other harvest their crops, and the women would gather to help one another finish pickling vegetables, share recipes, and gossip. I especially liked it when we all went to the Autry farm and then they, in turn, came to our farm. Even though Danny worked in the field with the adults, and Elizabeth and I helped take care of the little ones to keep them from getting underfoot, it was the only time during this busy season that I ever got the chance to spend time with Danny even for a few minutes, and I was grateful for it.

After the crops were harvested, Pa and Luke would take the corn and wheat to the gristmill to be ground into meal and flour. They usually made two or three trips in order to get all the corn and wheat ground. Pa and Luke would also make one special trip to take a few of our calves to town to sell to Greeneville's hotel and restaurant for money to buy supplies. But on the last trip the whole family would go into town with them. Ma, Elizabeth, Becky, Ben, and I would go to the general store to buy sugar, salt, material to make clothes, coffee, ammunition, and other supplies. Greeneville was a fairly large town with a general store combined with the post office, a church, a hotel and restaurant, a bakery, a small shoe shop, and a tavern. Ma strictly forbade any of us to go to the tavern because they sold liquor, although I think Pa and Luke slipped in there while we girls did our shopping.

Ma, Elizabeth, Becky, Ben, and I always visited the bakery and shoe shop first. I liked the bakery because they sold chocolate cookies and Ma would let me go in and buy all of us kids a cookie. Elizabeth's favorite store was the shoe store where she always succeeded in ruining our shopping trip with her continuous begging and whining. She knew full well that Ma would buy each of us kids one pair of everyday shoes and a pair of Sunday shoes if we had outgrown or worn out our old ones, and that was it. But, no, Elizabeth had to whine and cry and try to get Ma to buy her an extra pair.

"Ma, look at those adorable shoes! I just have to have them please, please, please! I know they made them just for me! Can't I have them? Please, Ma, please?" Then she would pout during the rest of our trip because Ma wouldn't let her have her way. Sometimes I just wanted to slap her!

Yet, despite Elizabeth's whining, I loved all the stores and the shopping! Our last stop, the general store, was filled with just about everything you could possibly want or need! Besides the essential supplies, there were toys, books, bolts of cloth for making clothes, big items such as plows and harnesses, guns and ammunition, dishes, and best of all, peppermint candy! Along with the cookie, we all got one piece of peppermint candy which we savored all the way home by making it last as long as possible.

When all the crops were in, all of the supplies bought, all the wood chopped, and everything preserved and stored, we would have huge community parties called harvestings with lots of food, fiddle playing, and dancing. Everyone would have a great time, and everyone had a great time this year, except me. For some reason around the time of my birthday, I began to feel different. I felt unsettled and not my usual, fun-loving self. The first thing I noticed was my loss of patience with my younger siblings. Ben and Becky were just naturally loud and rambunctious and normally I just ignored them or went down to the river for some peace and quiet. Now, I found myself yelling at them on a fairly regular basis. And Elizabeth! Oh my goodness! She drove me absolutely crazy with her endless chatter about boys and her whining about wanting a new dress, or new shoes, or something! I couldn't stand to be around her! Luke was about the only one of my siblings I could tolerate, and really I didn't want to be around him that much. Even Ma noticed and finally queried me as to the cause of my short temper. I asked, "What short temper?" She just gave me a funny, sort of knowing look and resumed putting the last of the apples in crates to store in the cellar.

Winter soon covered us under its light blanket of snow. Even when the snow stopped falling allowing the sun to timidly peek through the clouds, it was really too cold to do much outdoors except trudge to school and back home again and take care of the necessary chores around home. Ben and Becky were responsible for gathering eggs and feeding the chickens, Luke helped Pa take care of the cattle, and I fed and milked our faithful milk cow, Betsy, fed Bill and Buttercup, our horses, and our old mule, Gus, and helped with some of the housework. Elizabeth somehow managed to help Ma with cooking and housework despite her endless chattering and whining.

Christmas was a very special time of the year for our family. My grandparents, Grandpa and Grandma Russell, would travel all the way from their home on Bean's Creek in Franklin County to spend Christmas with us. Luke and I would give up our beds for Grandpa and Grandma and sleep on old straw mattresses on the floor. They would usually stay until right after the New Year and then head back home. I always thought that it must be nice to be old and go where and when you pleased. Then I thought about the "old" part and changed my mind. We always had a lot of fun with them, though. Grandpa loved to tell us stories. All of us kids would sit on the floor for hours while he sat in Ma's rocking chair in front of the fireplace and told us story after story about catching hundred-pound fish and fighting fifty-foot bears. Grandma loved to cook, so she and Ma made cakes and pies and cookies. Then, of course, there was the huge meal on Christmas Day. We always had turkey, cornbread stuffing, and pickled vegetables that we had put up from the garden, and all those lovely cakes and pies. My mouth always watered just thinking about the sweet, cinnamon aroma of fresh-baked hot apple pie, and the savory, oniony, smoky aroma of roasted turkey and dressing.

The day before Christmas Eve every year, Pa, Luke, and me went to cut a Christmas tree. We would search for hours for the perfect tree. After Pa chopped it down, I helped Luke carry it home. Pa would strap two pieces of wood to the base of the trunk for support and set it by the big window next to the front door. We kids would then make little stars and bows out of Ma's old scrap sewing material, and Ma would get out the few little special decorations and the star that had been handed down to her from

Grandpa and Grandma, and let Ben and Becky put them on the tree. After everyone had gone to bed that night, I would tiptoe into the living room and admire our beautiful tree illuminated by the dying glow of the fire. All the ornaments seemed to come alive with light as they dangled from the perfectly formed branches of the tree. I would close my eyes and inhale the pungent, piney aroma of those branches while listening to the cold wind sigh and moan around the corners of our warm, comfortable house. I always thought that Christmas tree was the most beautiful thing in the world. I loved Christmas!

Christmas Eve was a lot of fun too. The community always had a party at the community building. The men would move the church pews back to the schoolhouse part of the building, leaving a wide open space for dancing. Danny's pa played the fiddle and knew all the dance tunes. There would be tables and tables of food since every family brought at least one or two dishes. But the best part about this Christmas Eve was going to be wearing the Christmas dress Ma made me every year. Now I usually don't like to dress up, but for some reason this year, I wanted to look pretty. I had noticed last year that just about all of the teenage girls had wanted to dance with Danny, which didn't really bother me then because he was two years older and had dark, curly hair, blue eyes, and the "most adorable smile," according to my goofy, boy crazy sister. But for some reason, now it bothered me and I wanted to look my best.

"Elizabeth, will you help me fix my hair?" I begged.

"What's in it for me?" she countered with a sly, knowing look in her eyes, sensing that I was desperate and knowing she had the upper hand.

"Oh, I'll do your chores tomorrow," I said sulkily.

"I'll help you if you do my chores for a month."

"For a month! Oh, all right," I said through gritted teeth.

She went to work taming my long, curly hair and bending it to her considerable will, which, I could tell, took a lot of effort on her part. She also showed me how to pinch my cheeks and bite my lips to add color to them. When I looked into Ma's old mirror with the crack in the corner, I thought I looked kind of pretty. My green eyes sparkled above my pink cheeks, and Elizabeth had piled my curly hair on top of my head, leaving a few tendrils hanging down to frame my face.

"I can't wait for everyone to see me!" I exclaimed happily, and I noticed Ma giving me that funny, knowing look again.

It took us a while to get everyone ready and loaded into the wagon, but finally we were on our way to the Christmas Eve Dance. I fidgeted the whole way, which irritated Luke because he had to sit by me. By the time we arrived at the dance, several families were already there. I could see the glow of lanterns hanging from the rafters and a fire blazing in the building's large fireplace. People were milling around talking and eating, but the dance music had not yet begun.

Excitedly, I ran inside to find Danny. Frantically, I scanned the room and when I finally found him, my heart sank. He was with Sarah Collins, Rachel's younger sister, in the corner next to the fireplace. He was holding her hands and they seemed to be having a deep, intense discussion. Just then, Danny's pa struck up a tune on his violin, and Danny grabbed Sarah's hand and took her out on the dance floor. I froze, not knowing what to do, when, suddenly, Tommy Williams, a boy from school, grabbed my hand and we were whirling around the dance floor. Despite the small twinge of envy quietly growing in my gut at seeing Danny with Sarah, I thoroughly enjoyed dancing with Tommy.

When the dance ended, I looked around for Danny. Two other girls were already vying for his attention. I had to admit that he did look handsome with his blue eyes flashing in merriment, his black curly hair in a tussle, his shirt with two of the top buttons undone due to his exertion from dancing. Oh my goodness, what was I thinking! Then, on top of all that, inexplicable hurt and anger surged to the surface of my brain. I told myself I didn't care and danced with Jesse Burns, one of Luke's friends. Then I went to find out what Pa and the rest of the men were discussing by the punch bowl.

As usual, the men were talking politics. Mr. Williams was concerned about the land bill that Congressman David Crockett had assured everyone he could get passed this year. He had settled on some of the land that the state was planning to use to give to North Carolina soldiers for their service during the Revolutionary War when Tennessee and North Carolina were the same territory. "Has anyone heard anything about the progress of that land bill?"

"I haven't heard much, "Pa replied, "but I don't think it's getting very far."

"Dang! Where is Crockett? He promised he could get it passed!"

"He's trying his best. I heard he was stumping, and fighting for it most every day, but he don't get along with 'Old Hickory,' our esteemed President, and that definitely don't help his cause none. Now they say he is on a whirlwind tour of the country selling his books and being wined and dined by all the big shots in the country." Congressman Crockett had co-authored an autobiography about himself which proved to be quite popular with major actors performing plays based on the book.

"Has anybody heard anything about Sam Houston?" asked Mr. Burns.

My ears perked up in extreme interest at this question. Sam Houston was one of Tennessee's larger-than-life heroes. He had fought with President Andrew Jackson at the Battle of Horseshoe Bend. He had been badly wounded but survived and became a regional hero and political protégé of President Jackson, or Old Hickory, as he was most widely known in Tennessee. Everyone just knew that, one day, he would be president of the United States. Sam Houston had been elected governor of Tennessee in 1826 and had married nineteen-year-old Eliza Allen in January

1829. Although no one knows exactly what happened, Eliza left Governor Houston, causing him to resign as governor in April of that year, and went back to her family. According to the avid gossip which inevitably follows such an unfortunate event and travels like wildfire, poor Sam left Tennessee and went to live with the Cherokees. At least, that was the last bit of gossip I had heard.

"I heard Old Sam left the Indians and is now in DC trying to get people to buy land in Texas," offered up Mr. Williams.

Ooh, now that was interesting! Texas! I had heard a lot about Texas. It was a territory that belonged to Mexico, but the Mexican government had opened it up to American settlers because they couldn't get enough Mexican settlers to move there due to hostile Indian populations. A lot of Tennesseans had packed up and moved there to take advantage of the very inexpensive land. All you had to do was swear allegiance to the Mexican government and become a Catholic. Word was that Texas was a paradise of woods, rivers, rich farm land, and lots of game. I daydreamed about going there some day.

I soon became bored with their conversation and also forgot that I was angry with Danny. I went to search for him and finally found him at one of the food tables devouring most of a plate of fried chicken. I guess dancing with every girl at the party would make a man ravenous. I walked up to him and spoke coolly, "Hello, Danny."

He looked at me in surprise. "Wow! Hello, Samantha. Where have you been? You look amazing!"

"It's so kind of you to take time out of your busy dancing schedule to acknowledge my presence," I replied sarcastically.

He looked puzzled. "What's the matter with you? Oh, forget it. Come on. Let's dance."

We danced the last two dances of the evening together, and, by the end of the party, everything felt back to normal again. We were Danny and Samantha, best friends and partners in crime forever.

3

Christmas went by much too fast and soon Grandpa and Grandma headed back home. The house felt very empty after they left and we took down the Christmas tree. Then all that was left to look forward to were long, cold, winter days and trudging to school through what seemed like endless miles of snow. Pa would take us to school if it was snowing very hard, and if we had a heavy snow, school was cancelled. There was really not much to do during the winter. I begrudgingly did all of Elizabeth's chores even though I had to admit, she did a great job of making me look nice. Sometimes Pa and Luke would go hunting for squirrel or a deer so that we could have fresh meat for a change instead of the smoked meat we had stored for the winter. There were still the usual chores to do, but for the most part, our lives seemed to adopt the patterns and rhythms of nature now sleeping under its blanket of snow.

But the days of winter flew by and soon spring began to make its presence known. The snow melted, swelling the river to the very top of its bank, and sending it roaring past our house. School let out for spring planting so Danny and I always tried to sneak in a little fishing in the midst of all the planting and spring cleaning. But I spent most of those days helping Luke and Pa plow the fields with Old Gus in preparation for planting the corn and wheat, while Elizabeth helped Ma plant the spring garden and give the house a thorough cleaning. I loved spring. It was great to feel the warm sun on your face after the long, cold winter. I always got excited thinking about all the hunting, fishing, and skipping rocks on the swollen river that Danny and I would be doing now that we could get outside. But this year, for some reason, there were times when I would feel sad. I would think about the fun we had at Christmas with Grandpa and Grandma and miss them so badly that I began to cry. Then I would get back to plowing, which usually involved a fighting match with Gus to get him to plow straight rows, and forget why I felt sad. I felt very strange and silly, so I didn't tell anyone about my feelings, not even Danny.

Then *that* day arrived in May. Ma called it 'entering womanhood' and she seemed just overjoyed about it.

"Oh, Samantha," she cried with tears in her eyes. "I knew you were going to be a late bloomer, but now you are a beautiful, young woman!"

I was about as overjoyed as a pig stuck under a gate. I didn't feel very womanly or beautiful at all. In fact, physically and emotionally, I felt like a mess. I ran down to the river and just sat on the bank crying. Soon I felt someone put a hand on my shoulder and then sit down beside me. It was Danny. He had been picking blackberries down by the river and had come to see if I wanted to help. I just looked up at him and started bawling.

"Sam, what's the matter?" he asked, concern evident in his voice.

For a little while, I didn't speak. How could I tell Danny about this; it was so deeply personal. Then I wailed between sobs, "Oh Danny, I'm blooming, and I DON'T WANT TO BLOOM!"

He just looked at me funny, as if he had no idea what I was talking about. Then he started to laugh and wrapped his strong arms around me in a big bear hug.

"Oh, Sam, it's going to be all right," he said and just held me. I remembered then that he had two older sisters and that he not only understood, but had to live this nightmare vicariously through them.

I brought up this fact and he said, "Yea, that is usually when you and I do a lot of hunting and fishing...FAR AWAY FROM THE AUTRY HOUSE."

We both laughed and then the most wonderful thing happened. Danny kissed me. The funny thing about the whole experience was my lack of surprise. It was kind of nice and seemed like the perfectly natural thing to do. His lips were soft and gentle and tasted like fresh blackberries. What did surprise me were the feelings that began to stir deep in my stomach, which evolved into a kind of heated urgency that made me put my arms around him and kiss him longer. We finally pulled away and smiled at each other, then walked back to the house holding hands.

Although we never talked about the incident with anyone else or even between ourselves, things were definitely different between Danny and me. We didn't hunt or fish as much as we used to do. Mostly we just sat on the bank of the river and talked about our futures. I realized that I had fallen deeply in love with Danny and now my future was intertwined with his. He talked a lot about going to Texas, which made me very unhappy because I couldn't imagine leaving Ma and Pa. But now I also couldn't imagine living without Danny. Our problem was that Danny had turned sixteen last April, had finished school in May, and was now ready to move on with his life. I would turn fifteen in November and would finish school a year from now. I understood why Danny wanted to leave Tennessee. His older brother would inherit the Autry place after their father died, leaving Danny with no land, and Danny wanted land and a place to farm. His family had just received a letter from his uncle, Micajah Autry, who lived in Jackson, Tennessee, and was planning to join a group headed for Texas within the next year. Uncle Micajah said he had heard that Texas was a paradise.

Texas. We had been hearing quite a lot more about her lately. She was a territory of Mexico under the rule of the Dictator Antonio Lopez de Santa Anna. From what I had heard about

Santa Anna, he sounded like a very traitorous, tyrannical character. He had been elected President of Mexico in 1833 under Mexico's then republican government which had only recently won independence from Spain. He then threw out Mexico's Constitution of 1824 upon which its republican government had been established, and had appointed himself dictator of all Mexico, including its territories. This, of course, did not sit well with the settlers in Texas, who refused to bow down to a dictator. It all sounded very complicated and I wasn't too sure about going there and getting mixed up in what sounded like a huge hornet's nest to me. But if Danny was going to Texas, then I was going also.

Our problem was deciding when and how to leave. We decided to go after I finished school a year from now so that gave me some time to figure out how I was going to explain our plans to my parents. I broached the subject with my parents one evening at supper.

"Pa, Ma, what would you think about me going with Danny to Texas after I graduate next year?" A look of horror crossed Ma's face and Pa spluttered and almost choked on his food. They both looked at me as if I had lost my mind.

Finally, Pa said, very calmly considering the circumstances, "No, Samantha, you are *not* going to Texas. You and Danny can get married and stay right here."

"But, Pa, Danny wants to go where he can farm his own land, and we heard that you can get 177 acres of land for almost nothing in Texas if you become Catholic and serve in the Texian army. Some of Danny's friends are already on their way to Texas and we can stay with them until we can build a house of our own. And I promise we won't leave until I have finished school next year." But they were both horrified that I would have to become a Catholic and were convinced that I would be tortured and killed in some horrible way in that wild, unsettled place. In fact, I had heard there were many American settlers already in Texas who, along with the Mexican settlers already present, had established some very nice towns. But Pa and Ma could not be persuaded to change their minds.

Danny and I talked at length about going to Texas. All during the summer, we would sit by the river and discuss our options. I was very reluctant to leave without Pa and Ma's approval and Danny was just as determined to go to Texas. His family was not fond of the idea, but couldn't really stop Danny since he would be seventeen next year. I just couldn't imagine my life without Danny and so we decided that, after I graduated, we would leave notes for our parents explaining our decision and head for Texas.

The rest of that year was very bittersweet knowing that everything I did with my family would probably be for the last time. That spring I offered to help plow the fields for planting just so I could spend some time with Old Gus. Gus was a good mule and I was his favorite person. I always fed him carrots and he never balked with me like he did with Luke. Spring and summer flew by and soon it was time to harvest the wheat, corn, and vegetable garden. I worked especially hard helping Ma store vegetables just so I could spend as much alone time with her as possible. I also spent a lot of time riding Buttercup because I knew I couldn't take her with me to Texas. All of the harvestings that were held that year still stand out in my mind as the rowdiest, most fun parties I had ever attended. In my mind's eye, I can still see Elizabeth in her fanciest party dress, her blond curls bouncing around her pretty face, blue eyes flashing, and her cheeks flushed with excitement from dancing with all of the eligible boys. I made sure to spend as much time as possible hunting squirrels and rabbits with Luke, which was very difficult considering the amount of time he spent with Rachel Collins.

I asked him about Rachel Collins one day while we were out squirrel hunting, because I had the distinct impression there was going to be a wedding in the not-too-distant future.

"Luke, have you asked Rachel to marry you yet?"

He grinned and punched me in the arm. "Maybe," he said. "What's it to you anyway?"

"It doesn't make me any difference. I just think it's about time you asked for her majesty's hand since you spend every spare waking minute kissing up to her," I retorted. He punched me again, so I punched him back and ran home as fast as I could to avoid getting beat up. I was going to miss Luke very much and was really sad that I would miss his and Rachel's wedding.

But most of all, I spent a lot of time with Becky and Ben, mostly because I knew that when and if I ever saw them again, they would be grown. One day I took them down to the river to play. The wildflowers dotted the grass in vivid violet, pink, and white colors. Becky loved to pick flowers for the dinner table, and watching her squeal with delight as she found each perfect flower then carefully pick them with her chubby little fingers brought tears to my eyes.

"What's wrong, Sam? Why you cryin'?" she asked.

"It's nothing, Becky," I assured her. "I was just thinking about how much I love you and Ben."

"Oh. Why that make you sad?"

"It doesn't. I'm crying because you make me happy."

She just gave me a puzzled look and went back to picking flowers.

I noticed that Ben, who had been trying to skip rocks across the river, was getting a little too close to the edge of the bank, so I grabbed Becky's hand and we went to join him. Soon we were all three plunking rocks into the river, chasing frogs along the bank, and having a great time.

My fifteenth birthday came and went without any fanfare as usual. Soon Christmas time arrived, and with it my grandparents. I was so very glad to see them and spend this one last Christmas with them before going to Texas. I had to face the fact that this might possibly be the last Christmas I would ever spend with them, and this brought tears to my eyes. We spent the days before

Christmas baking all of the delicious pies and cakes, laughing, and telling old stories.

On Christmas Eve, Elizabeth and I helped each other dress for the dance. Ma had stated that since I had finally "bloomed" and become such a beautiful young lady, I would have to have a Christmas dress that befitted such a girl. I just rolled my eyes and agreed, reluctantly and with great resignation, because this meant that I would have to wear the dreaded corset. I had watched my mother and sister cinch each other into these instruments of torture for years, and dreaded the day that I would be forced to wear this garment in which you were supposed to live and function without breathing. The only positive thing that could be said about wearing a corset was that it did make your waist look smaller and your chest look more…"developed." After much effort and considerable complaining on my part, Elizabeth succeeded in cinching me into the dreaded garment. I slipped the beautiful new green dress Ma had made me over my head and Elizabeth buttoned it for me.

Next Elizabeth undertook the unenviable task of fixing my hair. She twisted my unruly curls into a knot piled high on my head and secured it with pins, leaving those soft curly tendrils hanging down to frame my face. I looked into Ma's old cracked mirror and, at first, did not recognize the girl looking back. That pretty girl could not be me! But it was. The green dress gave my eyes an emerald green color, and my cheeks glowed pink with excitement. Elizabeth squealed with delight at the success of her efforts to, once again, transform me into a pretty young woman, and Ma had tears in her eyes.

Ma and Elizabeth looked beautiful in their dresses just as they always did and Grandma looked the "grand dame" in her formal gray dress with the white lace collar. I could tell by the look of pride on Pa's and Grandpa's faces and Luke's grin that the Russell women were going to be the belles of the ball, even if it was just a plain country Christmas dance at a small church schoolhouse on the Nolichucky River.

Danny was waiting for me at the door when we arrived at the dance, but instead of just letting him whisk me away to the dance floor, I insisted on making a grand entrance with Ma, Grandma, and Elizabeth. Everyone oohed and ahhed over our dresses and several boys asked me to dance, but I only wanted to dance with Danny. And tonight, he only wanted to dance with me. He looked so handsome in his best shirt and pants and polished boots.

We danced and danced and between dances drank plenty of punch and ate lots of the delicious food that was always available at this affair. Looking around, I could tell that many of his old girlfriends were jealous of me receiving all of his attention.

"Gee, Samantha, aren't you going to let anyone else dance with Danny?" Sarah Collins complained. I just gave her a smug little smile and grabbed Danny's hand for the next reel. It was a magical night and one that I will never forget.

My grandparents celebrated Christmas and New Year's with us and then went back home. Now the long days of winter stretched endlessly ahead of us. Danny and I would meet by the river or after school if it wasn't snowing too badly to discuss our plans for going to Texas. We decided to leave the day after spring planting. That way, we would at least help our families get the crops in the ground before we left. I told Danny we would probably have to leave that night since my parents were totally against my going to Texas. Danny had sold some rabbit pelts last fall, and his Pa had sold four calves and split the money between him and his brother. Danny figured we would have plenty of money to get us to Texas and rent a place to stay if necessary.

We agreed to start gathering supplies such as beef jerky, some dried fruit, and some cornmeal to take to eat and store it at Danny's house. We figured we could supplement our meat supply with fresh game along the way. Danny would bring his rifle, pistol and ammunition, and of course blankets, clothes, and tools. I would bring my own blankets, clothes, the books Mrs. Gerrard had given me, my trusty slingshot...and my beautiful green Christmas dress. I just couldn't leave it behind. Besides, I would wear it at my wedding when we got to Texas. Danny would also bring his horse, Buster, for us to ride, and a pack mule to carry our supplies. The reality of what we were doing had not hit me yet. Even though we were planning and gathering supplies for the trip, it seemed almost as if we were kids again playing make-believe. It just didn't seem real.

But spring finally arrived and the family began the annual crop planting. I finished school that May and told Mrs. Gerrard good-bye, thanking her for all of her assistance with my education. She gave me a copy of Shakespeare and *The Iliad* which brought tears to my eyes, and I gave her a big hug.

"Remember, Samantha, never let your love of learning fade away."

I promised I wouldn't as I waved good-bye and walked home. We finished planting the crops the next day, the 15th of May.

That night I lay awake on my bed with my clothes packed listening for Danny to arrive. I had written a letter to Ma and Pa explaining that we were going to Texas and that I would write to them as soon as we got settled. Around midnight, I heard a horse nicker outside and knew Danny had arrived. Quietly I got up, gently kissed Ben and Becky, placed my letter on the kitchen table, then slipped out the door and swung up onto Buster behind Danny. Danny nudged Buster with his knees and off we rode into the darkness.

4

We traveled the rest of the night until right before dawn and stopped for a few hours of sleep. I didn't think I could sleep, with my emotions roiling and my stomach in knots from worrying about my family's reaction to my running away from home. But soon, exhaustion set in and I slipped into unconsciousness. Danny woke me up a few hours later. We ate some beef jerky and cold cornbread and set out again.

We traveled on roads as much as possible, but were forced to follow animal trails through some unsettled areas along the way. We would travel until almost dusk and then make camp. While Danny built a fire, I would take my slingshot and try to kill a couple of squirrels or rabbits before it got too dark. Most evenings, I was pretty lucky in this endeavor, and we would have fresh meat for supper. After supper we would be so exhausted that we would make a bed out of pine needles, spread our blankets out over it, and immediately fall asleep. I guess I should have been afraid, sleeping outdoors in unknown, unsettled places with the darkness and all of its wild inhabitants kept at bay only by the light of our small campfire. But with Danny I felt invincible. This was probably a good thing because looking back on it, I figure most kids at that age with any sense would probably have been scared to death.

By the end of the week, we reached Memphis. I had never seen such a big town with so many houses and stores. The town was bustling with activity as people scurried to outdoor markets or to the stores to buy and sell their wares. The streets through town were a muddy mess from all the horse and wagon traffic, and I watched in amusement as the well-to-do ladies in their expensive dresses and shoes tried to tiptoe across the wooden boards laid along the sides of the street in a futile attempt to avoid all the mud. Loud piano music and raucous laughter emanated from the saloon across the street. I was reminded once again how Ma sternly warned us to steer clear of saloons because they were bad places full of sin and vice. I wasn't sure what she was talking about, but she was so adamant and stern about it that I never asked. I was going to ask Danny about it, but suddenly, my attention was drawn to the most beautiful sight I had seen since leaving home.

"Look, Danny, an inn with a restaurant! Can we spend just one night there, please? I so very much wanted to sleep on a real bed."

Danny gave me an annoyed look as he paused to contemplate this idea since it would require him to spend some of his precious money. I understood that he hated the thought of spending any of his money, since we had no idea what emergencies or situations we might encounter on the trip, but the price for one night's stay per person was only fifty cents and that included supper and breakfast and twenty-five cents extra to stable Buster and the mule. Since it was evening and the sun was beginning to set, we rented a room with two beds. After eating a supper of beef stew and cornbread with apple pie for dessert, we went upstairs to our room where I luxuriated in the comfort of sleeping on a real mattress with a real pillow.

The next morning we arose early, went to the general store, bought some paper, ink, and two envelopes and came back to the restaurant to eat breakfast and write letters to our parents.

Twinges of guilt and remorse brought tears to my eyes as I wrote my letter. Wiping my eyes, I resolutely sealed it in my envelope, laid it by my plate, and focused all of my attention on our huge breakfast of bacon, eggs, biscuits, and grits. After breakfast, we dropped our letters off with the postmaster and went to the stable to collect Buster and our mule. Then we headed down to the river.

We were not far from the river when I witnessed a most awful sight. A large platform had been built not far from one of the docks, and on it stood a black man, woman, and two little boys in chains. Around the platform a group of white men waited eagerly to bid on the family as the auctioneer began his fast-paced, monotone sales pitch. I froze, unable to take my eyes off the horrible sight. The little boys were crying and, just then, the woman looked straight at me with a look of such fear and sadness that my heart lurched with pity and my eyes filled with tears of helplessness. Danny took my arm and guided me away toward the ferry dock. We didn't speak about the incident. I don't think we could because I could tell the sight of that family being auctioned off had upset him badly by the look of anger and pity in his eyes. The plight of that poor family would haunt me for as long as I lived.

I felt my eyes widen in wonder when we finally reached the ferry landing on the Mississippi River. I had never seen such a huge river! It must have been at least a mile across and so busy! It seemed to me like hundreds of boats and barges traveled up and down its deceitfully calm, muddy gray surface, for underneath the river's current proved strong and treacherous. It really was exciting to watch! Danny soon found a ferryman that was available to take us across for a reasonable price and soon we were on our way. Because of the strong current, Danny had to help the man paddle us across. I admired that river! It reminded me of a strong, beautiful gray stallion, which could never be properly broken and barely tolerated the insignificant humans endeavoring to use him for travel.

We finally made it across and were soon traveling across the Arkansas territory. I really liked the Arkansas Territory and probably could have settled there if Danny hadn't been so determined to go to Texas. We traveled through large areas of dense woods interspersed with acres of rolling farmland. It rained on us the first few days we were in Arkansas. Danny built us a makeshift lean-to out of pine branches and brush which wasn't very waterproof, but was better than sleeping on the wet ground with rain pouring on us.

Fortunately, on one of those rainy nights, we found a farm family, the Chapmans, who let us sleep in their barn out of the cold, damp weather. They also invited us to eat supper with them that night. It was so good to have a hot home-cooked meal for a change! I hate to admit it, but we ate like hogs. Ma would have been mortified if she had seen us. Mrs. Chapman just smiled and said, "I'm so very glad that some people appreciate all the hard work that goes into preparing meals around here."

Mr. Chapman just rolled his eyes and asked, "Where are you kids headed?"

"To Texas to either San Antonio or Gonzales," replied Danny. "I'm going to serve my time in the military and then we are going to claim our share of the land."

"Well, son, you may get the chance to do some actual fighting in Texas. Rumor has it that Ol' Santa Anna, that Mexican dictator, wants to start kicking Americans out of Texas. I hear things are starting to really heat up on the other side of the Red River."

Danny and I looked at each other apprehensively. That night we had a long discussion about whether we should keep going, but decided we had come too far to turn back now. We would continue on to Texas.

The next morning we thanked the Chapmans for their hospitality, gratefully accepted a biscuit with sausage for breakfast from Mrs. Chapman, and started out early. We had to cross the White River, and then the Arkansas River before finally reaching the Red River which formed the border between Arkansas and Texas. We found fairly shallow areas along the White River and the Arkansas River where Buster and the mule could wade across, and within another week's time we were standing on the bank of the Red River and getting our first look at our new home: Texas.

I tried to go to sleep after supper that night but couldn't.

"Danny, "I whispered, "are you awake?"

"I am now," he replied in a slightly annoyed voice. "What's the matter?"

"I can't sleep."

"No kidding," he said sarcastically. "Why can't you sleep?"

"I guess I'm too excited."

"Well, close your eyes and try to sleep anyway."

I hated when people said that. As if closing your eyes would automatically turn off your brain and put you to sleep. I mean, if that worked, I would be asleep already, wouldn't I?

After a little while, I whispered, "Danny, it didn't work. I still can't sleep."

I heard him give a long, irritated sigh. Finally, he said, "Come over here."

I scooted over next to him and cradled my head in the crook of his shoulder. Finally the soothing warmth of his body emanating through his clothes and the sound of his steady breathing put me to sleep.

The next morning, we boarded a ferry and crossed the Red River into Texas. The dark shadowy landscape created by the thick piney woods ahead of us looked somewhat forbidding, but we soon found a deer trail and began following it southwest. We traveled until almost dark and stopped to make camp for the night. While Danny took care of the animals and began preparing to build a fire, I took my slingshot and went in search of a couple of nice, plump squirrels.

Before I had gone too far into the woods, I thought I saw smoke rising above the trees about fifty yards ahead of me. I crept forward quietly and soon saw a large clearing ahead with cone shaped grass huts and heard voices and laughter. From the shape of the huts and the layout of the encampment, I recognized the Indians as Caddos. Pa knew a great deal about many of the Indian tribes in the United States and had told me about the Caddos. I always thought Caddo was a funny name and wondered where it came from. Anyway, I knew they were not very aggressive or easily provoked to violence unless threatened, so I crept a little closer being careful to stay hidden in the brush. I just watched them for a few minutes. The children ran and played while the adults cooked over fires, and prepared for nightfall.

Suddenly, I heard the crack of a limb in the thicket off to my left. I turned just in time to see a face framed with long dark hair emerge from one of its bushes. It was a Caddo Indian boy from the village ahead, and I think I startled him as much as he startled me. I saw his eyes widen in surprise as I let out a small scream and quickly backed out of the brush and ran back to camp.

Danny looked up in alarm as I came crashing through our camp, stumbled over a tree root, and fell into his arms.

"Samantha, what's wrong?"

"Caddo Indians," I gasped, "not far from here! One of them saw me!"

Even though we knew the Caddos were probably harmless, we figured the fact that they now knew we were in their territory might not sit well with them. We decided to travel a little farther that night before making camp. A full moon illuminated the landscape, and every bush and tree along the side of the road seemed to harbor sinister stalking shadows. Suddenly, we heard a branch crack under the feet of some large animal and a screech owl cry out as it swooped across the road. I jumped so violently that I nearly fell off of Buster, and Danny nudged him into a trot so we could put as much distance between ourselves and the Indian camp as possible.

I guess the Caddos did not consider us much of a threat because we did not see any more Indians that night. Even though we felt pretty sure we were safe, we were leery about building a fire. Mrs. Chapman had packed us some extra biscuits with sausages, which we ate before finally collapsing into a fitful sleep.

We awoke early the next morning and made it to the small, rustic town of Nacogdoches by noon. We didn't linger in Nacogdoches but I briefly glimpsed a small church, a general store, and a few log houses as we passed through. We found the El Camino Real (the Royal Road) outside of town and traveled along it all that day and half of the next before the trees began to thin out and the road began to cross prairies with grasses as high as Buster's belly. That day, we traveled as far as the Trinity River and made camp there. We didn't build a fire because we were still a little skittish after our encounter with the Caddo Indians. So that night, we ate some jerky and cold cornbread and fell asleep to the sound of the river whispering and gurgling along its banks, frogs croaking, and an owl hooting in the distance.

The next morning, we found a curve in the river not far from our camp where the river's travel had laid silt, forming a sandbar and narrowing the river. We crossed here and traveled until we came to the Brazos River. A man operating a ferry took us across to the settlement of San Felipe de Austin, the first Anglo settlement in Texas and its temporary capital. It was also a very rustic, lively little town with log buildings built around a central square. The town's main street circumventing the square and exiting the town proper was quite literally a ribbon of muddy mire formed by rain, horse manure, and continuous wagon traffic. The buildings lining the square housed a small store, a tavern, the law office of an attorney named William B. Travis, and what appeared to be a town hall. I could hear a lot of men talking and arguing in there.

From the angry voices emanating from the town hall, I could tell things were heating up against Mexico. I heard one man remark quite heatedly, "Santa Anna cannot be reasoned with. I know this because I tried and spent two years in a Mexican prison for my efforts!"

Another man agreed. "You tell 'em Stephen!"

"That must be Stephen F. Austin in there," exclaimed Danny excitedly. "He brought the first settlers from the United States to Texas!"

I just stared at the building with wide-eyed awe as we slowly rode past on our way through town. I would have liked to stay longer to find out why everyone was so upset, but Danny wanted to cover as many miles as possible before nightfall, so we kept going.

Even though we began to encounter more farms and settled areas, we remained wary and on our guard. We had heard that there were still several Indian tribes such as the Tonkawas, the Lipan Apaches, and the Comanches, who did not exactly approve of white settlers moving into their territory. We continued on until almost nightfall and made it to the Colorado River. So far we had had no further encounters with or seen any signs of Indians. So we made camp, killed a couple of rabbits for supper, and ate the rest of our cornbread and some dried fruit. I felt like I had had a feast after eating jerky the past two days.

After supper as we were enjoying the warmth of a fire, we decided it was time to decide which town we would choose for our new home since we were now in areas more populated by settlers. Surprisingly, we didn't have a very long discussion. I loved the idea of settling in San Antonio de Bexar with its old-world Spanish charm which I had heard was quite beautiful. But Danny's friends had settled in Gonzales, and we figured we would probably need all the help we could get with, first of all, finding temporary lodging, and second, negotiating the complexities of obtaining land. Danny's good friend from back home, William Summers, lived just north of Gonzales. He had written to Danny just before we left Tennessee and had invited us to live with him in his two-bedroom log home until we could get settled. So we agreed that Gonzales would be the location of our new home. It took us another day and a half to finally make it to Gonzales. I was so excited and eager to get there that that day and a half seemed to last forever.

By not stopping for a midday meal, we arrived at William's farm just after noon. William greeted us exuberantly with a bone-crushing hug and a huge grin. "Danny, I thought you two would never get here! What took you so long? It's just a hop, skip, and a jump from here to Tennessee." We both laughed partly at his jest, but mostly in relief that the long trip had finally ended. After we had unpacked and taken care of the animals, William showed us his farm. He had cleared fifty acres of his land on which he had built his house, a barn, and a small smokehouse. He had fenced off twenty acres for his cattle, had planted twenty acres in cotton for a cash crop, and had a small garden growing next to his house. I was impressed! Most of Danny's friends, or at least the ones I had known, had always been kind of lazy. William definitely was not! After our tour, William decided we should go into town and meet everyone. I couldn't help feeling a little nervous about this. After all, I was just a country girl from Tennessee and had had very limited social interactions outside of my family and immediate friends.

I soon found out I had nothing to worry about. The tiny town of Gonzales sat unobtrusively on the banks of the Guadalupe River. Due to its size, the townspeople were very down-to-earth country folk who were very eager to get to know all newcomers and make them feel welcome. Therefore, our arrival caused quite a stir and provided the town with an excuse to have a party. Before I knew it, some of William's friends had herded us into the tavern where a curious crowd soon gathered to see what all the excitement was about. Mrs. Johnson, whose husband owned the tavern, brought out bread and cheese and Mr. Johnson began serving drinks. Then someone brought out a fiddle and the party began!

I had just begun conversing with some of the ladies, when an older gentlemen with only two front teeth grabbed me around the waist and whirled me across the dance floor. I looked around desperately for Danny to come and rescue me. This proved to be a futile effort since he was too busy drinking at a corner table to notice. So I smiled at my toothless partner and resolutely finished the dance. He turned out to be a pretty good dancer, which reinforced Pa's old adage that you can't judge a book by its cover.

After being asked to dance with most of the male members of the community, which I really didn't mind because I loved to dance, I managed to escape and make my way over to Danny and William's table. Much to my disgust, Danny and William had become quite intoxicated, which placed me in the position of having to haul them home in William's wagon and get them to bed. I made a point of getting up extra early the next morning and making quite a lot of noise cooking breakfast.

After breakfast, Danny and I went exploring on horseback to determine where we might decide to settle. We found a 177 acre parcel of land by the river about ten miles north of town. The land seemed so very flat compared to our land of rolling hills in Tennessee. But it was good farming land and contained large stands of oak trees and a few pecan trees. The one drawback was that it was covered in brush and would take a lot of work to clear it for farming.

We rode back to town, filed a claim at the land office, and paid only $7.08 for the entire property. It was hard to believe such good farmland could be so inexpensive! We would have to wait a while for the claim to be approved, but the land officer told us that he foresaw no complications with the approval due to the fact that the first claimant to the property had forgone his rights to the land because of the escalating tensions with Mexico and had moved back to Arkansas. The land office also served as the army enlistment station and since all the men were required to join their local military unit, Danny enlisted with J.C. Neill's artillery unit.

The next day we visited the tiny church on the edge of town in the midst of a grove of oak trees. It was a beautiful, small, whitewashed building with a single stained glass window depicting the Virgin Mary holding Baby Jesus. There was a small cemetery behind the church surrounded by a neatly whitewashed wooden fence. A beautiful live oak grew in the center of the cemetery under which a log bench had been placed for people who wanted to visit loved ones buried there. This picturesque, serene place provided such a stark contrast to the hustle and bustle of the busy little town of Gonzales.

Danny and I had decided we wanted to become Catholics and be married as soon as possible. Now I realized that, at the age of fifteen, I didn't know very much about the ways of the world, but I knew I loved Danny. We had spent so much time together on this trip to Texas, and he had been so patient, gentle, and cool-headed, even when I was impatient, irritable, and anxiety-ridden, which was quite often, I might add. I knew he loved me or he wouldn't have put up with me and, in my eyes, he was perfect. Besides, I would be sixteen in a few months anyway, and Ma had told me that she was sixteen when she and Pa married.

We found a parishioner cleaning the church. We introduced ourselves and inquired about the whereabouts of the priest. "Oh, Father Hidalgo has to travel from San Antonio to Gonzales, and only comes twice a month to conduct services," Maria, the parishioner told us. "But you two are in luck. He will be in town this coming Saturday and Sunday."

We returned on Saturday, and found the priest preparing for the next day's services. We hesitated at the door of his tiny office not wanting to disturb him, but he glanced up from his work with a big smile, "Come in, my children. How may I assist you?"

Danny explained that we wanted to join the church and get married. Since he would not be back for two more weeks, he agreed to baptize us and conduct our wedding ceremony the next day on the condition that we would agree to faithfully attend church services whenever they were held. We agreed and were baptized and married the very next day, July 2, with the entire town of Gonzales as our wedding guests. I wore my green Christmas dress and William gave me away. I couldn't help feeling guilty that Pa wasn't there to perform this rite of passage with me, but consoled myself with the fact that he still had Elizabeth and Becky to give away in marriage. The women of the congregation had prepared a delicious picnic lunch to be eaten on the church grounds afterward which gave us the opportunity to properly meet and get to know everyone. The day couldn't have been more perfect, and I was the happiest person in the world because I was finally Mrs. Daniel Lee Autry.

That night after all the celebrating had ended and Danny and I were home alone, I sat in one of the kitchen table chairs feeling a little nervous. William had generously agreed to stay in town with friends so that we could have the house to ourselves, and suddenly I now realized that I had been so caught up in the excitement and romance of becoming a bride, I had never really given any thought to what it meant to be a wife. Danny and I had been the best of friends for most of our lives, but now I wondered how being married would affect our relationship.

Danny came into the cabin after taking care of the animals, his smile changing to a look of concern when he saw me sitting at the table looking worried. "Samantha, what's wrong?"

"I'm not sure…" I began, looking up at him anxiously. Finally, I just blurted it out, "I don't think I know how to be a wife."

Danny looked puzzled. "What do you mean you don't know how to be a wife? You can cook and take care of a house. You've been taking care of me. We grew up together and traveled across the country together, so I believe we know each other pretty well. I don't understand."

"I know…" I was finding it hard to explain how I felt. "But now that we're married, we're supposed to live as husband and wife, and I'm not sure I know what that means, how I'm supposed to act. Ma told me some things but I always got the feeling she was leaving something out, and when I would ask Elizabeth about being married, she would just giggle and turn red and be her totally useless self. I just don't want to mess things up by being ignorant."

Danny just smiled and pulled me out of the chair and into his arms. "My darling Sam, you could never mess anything up," he whispered into my ear. He kissed me softly at first, then more urgently, creating that familiar warm feeling in my stomach and arms that made me want to hold him and never let him go. I realized then that getting married had changed our relationship. It had changed from a love as friends into a stronger love in which two people become one.

The remainder of the summer flew by. When we were not helping William with the chores around his place or Danny was not training with his artillery unit, we were clearing our land. I used the machete to clear the smaller bushes and Danny cut down the trees. By the beginning of August, we were ready to start building our house and barn. We decided to start small and build a one-bedroom house not far from the river and a small barn just large enough to hold hay and shelter the animals. By using the trees that Danny had cut down clearing our land, and with the help of his army buddies, our little log house and barn were completed by late September.

It was a small one-room cabin with a large fireplace on the north wall, a window and door on the west wall facing the fields, and a window on the east wall facing the river. The fireplace was very special because Danny had built a small brick oven in the fireplace's right side wall. My mother had one in our fireplace in Tennessee. She would build a small fire in the oven to heat it up, then scrape the coals out of the little oven into the fireplace, put her bread into the little oven and let the oven's heated bricks bake the bread. Pa later bought her a wood cooking stove, but I knew I would not have that luxury for a quite a while. I would have to be content with my little oven and a cooking spit on which I could roast meat or hang a cooking pot. Our only furniture was a small table, two chairs, and a bed that William had given us for a wedding present. We put up a curtain to form a makeshift wall that separated our sleeping area from the living area. Our little cabin was very cozy and perfect for the two of us. It turned out to be a very good thing we finished it, because unbeknownst to us, the winds of rebellion had begun to blow.

5

Before we knew it, it was harvest time. Danny helped William pick his cotton crop and I spent my time pickling vegetables from William's garden. William had agreed that if we helped him harvest and put up vegetables for the winter, we could keep enough of the vegetables to get us through the winter until next spring when we could plant our own crops. Danny and William were also going to slaughter a pig later in the fall and smoke it, so that between pork and whatever deer we killed, we would have plenty of meat. There were a lot of deer around Gonzales, especially on our land. Also, one of the farmers who owned a large farm outside of town grew wheat, ground it, and sold it in town. Danny and I bought a few bags of flour and a milk cow. Now I had everything I needed to bake bread and biscuits.

On the days when we weren't helping William, Danny and I worked on plowing up our land for next year's crops. I loved those days, because it was just Danny and I working together. At the end of the day, he would be washing up down by the river, and I would sneak up behind him and push him into the water. He always managed to grab my dress and drag me in with him. We would laugh and splash around for a while. Then he would begin to kiss me, gently at first, then more urgently as he picked me up in his strong arms and carried me back to our cabin. We loved each other very much and were so very happy.

During the next few weeks, the winds of rebellion strengthened into a full-fledged storm with Gonzales directly in its path. Everyone in Texas had heard about how Santa Anna had destroyed the Mexican Constitution of 1824, made himself dictator of Mexico, and had butchered his own people in Zacatecas just because they opposed his unlawful actions. Danny went into town one day to buy some supplies from Adam Zumwalt's store and found out that Jesse McCoy, who worked for Mr. Zumwalt, had been bludgeoned to death the day before by a Mexican soldier.

Everyone was horrified and confused. Gonzales had always had a good relationship with Mexico and had even named the town after the governor of Coahuila y Tejas, Rafael Gonzales. After this incident, Danny forbade me to go into town without him or William. This upset me quite a bit, because I had made several friends in town, and enjoyed meeting with them and Mrs. Johnson at the tavern for coffee whenever I could get a break from working on the farm. Even though I loved Danny and liked William, sometimes I just needed to visit with women. I was discovering that men can be very obstinate and dense about many things, which was something I never realized until I married Danny.

A few days later, one of Santa Anna's generals, Colonel Ugartechea, rode into town demanding that we return the cannon Mexico had given us for protection from the Indians. Needless to say, the town went into an uproar. Andrew Ponton, our mayor, called a town meeting which turned into a very heated affair. When Mayor Ponton asked what should be done, one man shouted, "We'll give'em that cannon...one cannonball at a time!" At that, the entire room erupted in cheering and yelling.

Sure enough, later that week Colonel Ugartechea sent Lieutenant Castaneda with one hundred dragoons to retrieve the cannon, and the men of Gonzales beat them up and ran them out of town. Colonel Ugartechea, needless to say, was not happy about this whole affair, and, sure enough, Castaneda's troops returned to get the cannon. There were only eighteen men in town at the time to defend it, so Captain Albert Martin told the Mexicans that Mayor Ponton was out of town, and that the Mexicans must wait on the other side of the river for his return to negotiate the return of the cannon. In the meantime, the men of Gonzales buried the cannon and sent messengers to the nearby farms to gather men for battle. Danny and I were clearing a field when we saw the cloud of dust on our dirt road signaling an approaching rider.

"The Mexicans are coming to take the cannon!" he yelled excitedly. "We need all able-bodied men to assemble in the town square as soon as you can!"

Danny ran into the house and grabbed his rifle, while I ran to the barn to saddle Buster. As Danny jumped into the saddle, he commanded, "Samantha, you stay here and wait until I get back, and don't argue!"

I realized that arguing would be futile and not fair to Danny since he had enough to worry about right now. "All right," I agreed reluctantly. I hated to see Danny ride off not knowing if he would be okay.

My sensitive, loving husband, knowing the turmoil that I was feeling and seeing it reflected on my face, paused to reassure me. "Don't worry, Sam, I'll be all right." Then he leaned down, kissed me, and rode away. I finished clearing some more of the south field then spent the night pacing the floor wondering what was happening in Gonzales. Finally, I could stand it no longer. The next morning I rode our old mule into town.

When I arrived, I found that a squad of men from town had dug up the cannon and the townspeople were gathering metal scraps to use for canister because there were no cannonballs. Everyone was also readying their rifles and shotguns. I helped gather scraps for the cannon, then went to find Danny figuring he would be with Captain Neill's artillery company under Colonel Moore. I had met Captain Neill, but not Colonel Moore. He seemed to me to be a stern, imposing figure, and I determined that it would be prudent to avoid running into him at all costs. Unfortunately, at that moment prudence deserted me, and I ran to greet Danny who was busy making ammunition for his rifle. Danny was definitely not happy to see me.

"Samantha, what the heck are you doing here! I told you to stay at the house!" I could tell he was angry with me because his voice shook with fury. I had never seen Danny that angry, but I didn't back down.

"Well, you know I don't mind very well and it's too late to send me back home," I retorted, my chin jutting stubbornly in the air. I spent the night in town at the tavern, far away from Captain Neill's command and Danny's fierce anger.

The next day, I arose early and went in search of Danny's unit. The fog was very thick that morning and it took me a while to find them. I finally found them on Ezekiel William's farm across the river watching the Mexican army which had taken a position on a hill not far from the river. As I hid in the brush near the water's edge, I saw Danny with his fellow compatriots emerge from the brush and begin firing on the Mexicans. The report of all their rifles was so deafening I had to cover my ears. I could hear my heart pounding as loud as the rifle fire as I stared in fear, unable to move or speak watching the Mexican cavalry charge and the men from Gonzales quickly retreat back to the brush along the riverbank.

Then, surprisingly, the Mexican cavalry also began to retreat back to their original position. It took me a moment to figure out the reason—the thick fog blinded the soldados making it difficult for them to distinguish friend from foe. A standoff seemed inevitable, so under a flag of truce Colonel Moore met Lieutenant Castaneda in the middle of the battlefield. Their discussion must have proved unsuccessful because, just then, one of the boys from Danny's platoon raised a white banner emblazoned with a black cannon and the words "Come and take it," and Lieutenant

Colonel Wallace ordered Captain Neill to fire the cannon at the Mexicans. A very tense moment followed as silence fell over the field after that pivotal cannon shot, and we waited to see what the Mexicans would do.

Unable to stand the tension any longer, several of the men from Goliad including Danny's platoon began chasing the Mexican Army back toward the river. I couldn't stop myself! I ran after them to see what would happen when they all reached the river. I couldn't believe what happened next. The Mexicans literally plowed through that river in their hurry to get back across! The roaring splash of the water echoed eerily through the dense fog. They only slowed down once they had made it across. Then they regrouped into somewhat more orderly lines and headed back toward San Antonio de Bexar without their precious cannon.

I had never heard such yelling and cheering as that which traveled across that river dogging the footsteps of that humiliated Mexican Company. Granted, our victory against the Mexicans that day was a small one, but you would have thought we had won a war if you could have witnessed the celebrating that ensued. Someone started playing a fiddle, and before we knew it, it seemed like everybody in town was drinking and dancing in the street. Danny and I joined in for a while but finally started heading home late that night. We both fell asleep immediately, totally exhausted by the events of the past few days.

The next morning, I got up and cooked breakfast. Danny ate his breakfast in silence and then went out to clear some more land. I could tell he was upset and I was pretty sure I knew why. After cleaning up the kitchen, I went out to find him to ask if he wanted to talk. When I did find him, I almost decided to forget talking to him and head back to the house. He was chopping down a tree with such ferocity that bark was flying ten feet in every direction. I called his name as I cautiously approached.

"Danny?" I asked tentatively. "Do you want to talk?"

"I'm not in the mood to talk right now, Samantha," he answered tersely. "We'll talk at supper."

I could tell he was very angry with me, so I quickly headed back to the house. I finished my chores, worked on storing away our share of the pickled vegetables, apples, and dried peaches from William's garden and orchard in our small cellar beneath the house, and began to cook supper. Danny came home around dusk and we sat down to eat. The silence was deafening. Finally, I could stand it no longer.

"Danny, I know you're angry with me for going into town after you had told me to stay here. And I tried to stay, but I couldn't stand it, wondering what was happening and whether you were okay. I'm sorry, I just couldn't do it." I gave him my most pathetic look hoping it would soften him up a little. From the furious glare he gave me when he looked up from his plate, I could tell it hadn't worked.

"Samantha!" he snapped loudly. "You have got to understand that with everything that is going on right now, you have to listen and do as I ask. It's for your safety, my safety, and the men in my unit. It's hard enough to concentrate on what I am supposed to be doing in the middle of a battle without worrying about what impulsive, hare-brained idea you might decide to act upon and get yourself killed! Samantha, you are fearless, and I have always loved that about you. But you have got to learn that you are not indestructible, and until you finally get that fact through your beautiful, hard head, you are going to have to trust my judgment and do as I ask," he finished in a softer tone.

I realized he was right. "I know, Danny, and I'm sorry. I just couldn't help myself. I love you so much, and if anything happened to you, I don't know what I would do." By then, I had started to cry. He came around to my chair and took me in his arms.

"I know," he said softly into my hair, his chin resting on top of my head, "and you know I feel the same about you. That is why I got so furiously angry with you. Promise me you won't do that again." I swallowed hard and promised. Then together we cleaned up the dishes and went to bed.

After that, things returned to normal, both for us and the town of Gonzales. Everyone finished harvesting their crops and gardens and getting ready for winter. I soon found out that winters in Texas would be nothing like winters in Tennessee. There was no snow and only a few weeks of freezing weather. But autumn along the Guadalupe River was truly beautiful. All of the trees seemed to have donned "Joseph's coat of many colors" with their brilliantly colored leaves.

The town did have a two-day celebration to mark the end of a successful harvest season and the fact that the Mexicans had decided to leave us alone, at least for now. Adults and children participated in games and races during the day, and danced until the wee hours of the morning to great fiddle music. The women of the town kept the food tables filled with delicious food and the celebration closed on Sunday with everyone attending church service. It was a joyous event and everyone had a great time. Unfortunately, good, peaceful times such as these would not last much longer.

The second week of October marked a serious escalation of the tensions between us and Mexico. Danny and William had slaughtered a pig two days ago and had it curing in William's smokehouse, and Danny and I had decided to go into town to pick up some last-minute winter supplies. The town seemed to be overflowing with strangers, and I saw a large group of men congregated outside of the church. Just at that moment, Stephen Austin rode up to join the group. I couldn't believe it! The "father of Texas," as he came to be known, was standing right in front of me. Danny hurried to join the group when he saw Captain Neill speaking with his commander, Colonel Moore. I also noticed two other men who exuded a very commanding presence among the assembly. Danny later told me their names were William Travis and James Bowie, men with whom I would become well acquainted in the next few months. The men slowly filed into the church, all talking animatedly amongst themselves.

"Sam, you go ahead and get the supplies," Danny instructed. "I'll meet you later after I see what is going on."

I slowly walked over to the store, my mind racing. What could have happened that would instigate such a large meeting of so many important men? I asked Mr. Zumwalt if he knew what was going on.

"Not sure, Samantha, but I do know I haven't seen this many people in town ever! I did overhear one of the men say that the Mexican Army is headed for San Antonio de Bexar. So I guess they're trying to decide what to do about it."

Fear gripped my heart at his words, knowing this probably spelled serious trouble. I thanked him for the information, bought our supplies, and waited impatiently by the wagon for the meeting to adjourn.

When Danny emerged from the meeting, I could tell by the serious look on his face that the news probably wasn't good. It wasn't. Santa Anna's brother-in-law, General Cos, had brought a large contingent of Mexican troops into Texas and now occupied the town of San Antonio de Bexar. The men had elected Stephen Austin commander of the Texian forces and were calling for all able-bodied men to march to Bexar to fight Cos.

"I've got to go, Sam," Danny said softly as he watched the tears roll down my face. "I'll be okay."

"Promise?" I managed to ask between sniffles.

"Promise." He smiled. "And I'll write if I can or get word to you somehow. Besides, I'm sure messengers will be bringing word of how things are going back to Gonzales on a pretty regular basis." This was true. Word seemed to travel pretty fast between Goliad, Gonzales, San Felipe, and San Antonio de Bexar.

That afternoon, Danny gave me instructions on how to finish up getting things on our farm ready for the winter, packed his belongings, and made ammunition for his rifle. We ate our supper in silence and went to bed early. I drove Danny into town in the wagon the next morning, and watching him march off with his company was the hardest thing I believe I have ever done.

I was totally despondent for the next few days and just sat staring out of the window except when it was time to feed the livestock. Finally, I realized that I was neglecting things and roused myself to finish winter preparations. Danny and I had just finished cutting one last bunch of grass for hay and loading it in the wagon before we received word about the meeting. I needed to get it inside out of the weather, so I dragged myself out to the barn and pitched it inside. All of the smoked meat and pickled vegetables and fruit were stored away, and now I had nothing to do but mope and worry. We had a good frost by the end of October and a few freezes in November, but of course no snow. I realized that soon, it would be December and Christmastime, so I decided to write Ma and Pa and update them on all of the events that had occurred since Danny and I arrived in Texas. I didn't think they were going to be very pleased with our marriage and was very glad that Tennessee and Texas were very distant from each other. I had brought my books Mrs. Gerrard had given me and tried to read, but couldn't seem to concentrate. I just spent my time staring out the window, waiting for some word from Danny.

Two weeks went by and I could stand it no longer. I saddled Buster and rode into town to see if there had been any news. Sure enough, a messenger named John Jacobson had arrived the day before with news. Mr. Johnson, knowing how starved we all were for news, decided to take advantage of this fact and expounded at great length about the battle's events and gory details. From what I could gather from his rambling oratory, the Texians had reached San Antonio de Bexar and had found General Cos and his army firmly entrenched within the town. Not knowing what to do, Austin had sent Bowie and his men on a scouting mission to find a suitable place for a base of operations from which to plan their next moves. Bowie found Mission Concepcion which was located on a horseshoe shaped branch of the San Antonio River, and positioned his men around both arms of the horseshoe, forming a neat little trap. General Cos learned that Bowie was separated from Austin and decided to attack which turned out to be a big mistake on his part. The Mexicans, advancing across open field, were decimated by Bowie's troops hidden in the tree line along the arms of the horseshoe. They beat a hasty retreat back to Bexar to regroup and "lick their wounds" as John described it.

Finally, a woman asked the question I had been dreading, "How many Texians were killed?"

"Only one and his name was Richard Andrews," John reported. Andrews wasn't from Gonzales, and you could almost hear a collective sigh of relief at this news. But we all felt sorry for Andrews and his family.

Despite the bad news about Richard Andrews, it seemed this conflict would soon be over and our boys would be coming home. All that was left for them to do was to take Bexar and, after hearing about the victory at Concepcion, it seemed this would be an easy chore. Upon hearing John's news, the old men took him to the tavern for a celebratory drink while the women stood outside the general store chatting in excited relief. It seemed Danny's return was only a matter of time.

But Danny didn't come home soon, so I could only assume that things were not going as well as we all thought. Three weeks passed and, still, we received no news. November's arrival brought some very cold weather. I soon discovered that, even though it didn't snow, Texas "northers" could be raw, wet, cold, and miserable. I didn't get a chance to ride into town every week because of the weather and chores around the farm, but I was finally able to make the trip into town on my birthday. Just as I tied Buster up in front of the store, John rode into town with news.

Once again John felt obliged to expound at great length in order to make the most of his position as the center of everyone's attention. Therefore, I will include the abbreviated version as much as I was able to piece together from his coma inducing droning. According to John, although the Texians were beating Cos's army in minor skirmishes such as the one at San Patricio and the Nueces Crossing, Austin had no idea how to penetrate Cos's superior reinforced position at Bexar. The men wanted to attack, but Austin knew this would be a bad mistake due to Cos's superior numbers, and so many men had begun to desert.

John had also learned that the Texian government, which had been in a state of confusion for quite a while, had finally met on November 3 at San Felipe and formed a provisional government that voted to make Texas a state within the country of Mexico. It elected Henry Smith as governor and appointed Sam Houston as commander-in-chief of the regular army even though Austin was still in command outside of San Antonio de Bexar. Sam Houston...that name sounded familiar. As James droned on about how the fight for Texas seemed to be falling apart, I racked my brain trying to remember where I had heard that name. Oh yes, our former governor of Tennessee, the Christmas party, and Pa talking about how Houston had resigned because of a scandal and disappeared presumably to Texas. Well...now we knew. He had come to Texas and was making quite a name for himself. I would have to write Pa and tell him about this. My mind refocused on John and what he was saying. If men kept deserting at Bexar, maybe Austin would give up fighting and things could just go back to the way they had been...and Danny could come home.

After three more weeks of tense waiting and endless worrying, Danny did come home. The day was cold and gray, and I was outside feeding the livestock when I happened to glance up and see a lone figure walking across our southern field. I had to shield my eyes to keep them from watering from the biting wind as I tried to make out who was coming. Then my heart leaped in my chest, and I took off running toward him. I realize it sounds nauseatingly romantic, but I couldn't help myself. I threw myself into his arms, and he held me for so long I thought he would never let me go, which would have been okay with me.

We walked back to the house where I proceeded to give him a proper wife's welcome. Then I put a pot of water on to boil for coffee, and we sat down at the kitchen table. As we drank our coffee, Danny filled me in on what finally happened at San Antonio de Bexar. The Texians took the town, but it was quite a battle. According to Danny, on December 5, Captain Ben Milam, who had been appointed by Austin to lead a company of spies for the Texians, finally got enough of waiting to take Bexar and obtained permission to ask for volunteers to go with him to take the town. Danny described Milam as a very confident, charismatic character who demanded, "Who will follow old Ben Milam into San Antonio?" Out of five hundred Texians, three hundred agreed to go with Ben. Danny volunteered to go, but Captain Neill refused to let him go. Milam had told Neill that he needed them to move their artillery near a crumbling old mission called the Alamo and fire their cannons to create a diversion while he and the three hundred men stormed the town.

"I was pretty scared," Danny said, "because we had to move across the river into enemy territory. We were so close I could see the buttons on the Mexican's uniforms as they patrolled the streets of Bexar. If you want to know the truth, Sam, I was glad I didn't have to go with those volunteers. Those streets looked real small and closed in with all those Mexican soldiers marching around."

I felt sorry for Danny. I knew that even though he felt relief at not being allowed to go with Milam, he felt guilty for not being part of the attack force. "Danny, without your company's artillery support, Milam wouldn't have been successful," I reassured him.

"I know, but the Texians were fighting the Mexicans from house to house! That's how intense the fighting was! And we were winning! Finally, in desperation, Cos sent out a force from the town to attack the Texians who had stayed outside of town thinking Milam's force would leave to go to their defense. Colonel

Neill gave the order to fire and we buried them with cannon shot. They scurried back inside the town like a bunch of scared rats," Danny said proudly. "Cos finally surrendered on December 9 and is headed back to Mexico. So now San Antonio de Bexar is ours!"

"That's the best news ever!" I exclaimed. Then I saw the look on Danny's face. "Okay, what's the bad news?" I asked apprehensively.

Danny sighed and was quiet for a moment, then said, "You remember that old crumbling mission I told you about, the Alamo? Well, Colonel Neill has been assigned to defend it and San Antonio de Bexar even though we really don't think the Mexicans will be back for a while, if at all. I am going to have to go back to San Antonio."

I just looked at him for a few moments first in disbelief, and then finally with determination. "I'm going with you," I said. Danny didn't protest, probably because he had just gotten home and didn't want to argue. I knew we would get into it later.

Since there were plenty of single men in the company who had remained with Colonel Neill in San Antonio, the married men were allowed to stay home and spend Christmas with their families. Danny and I cut down a pine tree, and I decorated it with bows made from strips of material I had bought in town. It made our little cabin look like a picture of a perfect country Christmas, and my heart kind of ached thinking about my folks back in Tennessee and imagining the Christmas they were celebrating there. At least, I hoped they were, and then I felt guilty because they were probably missing me. I had received a letter from Ma a couple of weeks ago. She said they were all doing well and that Ben and Becky were growing like weeds. Luke and Rachel were getting married next month, and Elizabeth had finally decided who she wanted to marry from among her many beaus, and was engaged. Ma said that she and Pa were still not very happy with me, but that they were glad Danny and I were doing well. I was quite relieved to get that letter, and told myself I would write again when we got settled in San Antonio.

I was quite proud of my Christmas dinner. We had smoked ham, vegetables, biscuits, and a pecan pie. William came over and ate with us. He was supposed to be in San Antonio but was granted leave to attend to some personal business and help his sick parents back in Louisiana. I knew his parents had contracted cholera and were getting better but needed some help on their farm. William didn't go into any details about his "personal business" part, and I kind of doubted that he had any except for spending a little extra time with his girlfriend, Anne, who was still in Louisiana. Anyway, it wasn't any of my business, and I liked being around William. He always told funny stories that kept me laughing so hard my sides hurt.

Danny was a little apprehensive about me going with him to San Antonio, but Colonel Neill had assured him that the Mexicans probably wouldn't be back, and if they did come back, it wouldn't be until the spring. Also, I begged and pestered him until he finally gave in and agreed to let me come along. We boarded out the milk cow to Mr. Carson, whose farm was adjacent to ours, on the condition that he could use the cow to help provide milk for his family. Then we cleaned out the fireplace, boarded up the windows on the house, closed up the house and barn, and loaded the belongings we were taking onto the mule.

6

We arrived in San Antonio on January 6, 1836. I fell in love with San Antonio de Bexar the moment it came into view just below a slight rise upon which we had paused before entering town. The sun had just begun to set, casting a coral glow upon the town, softening the lines and colors of its old world architecture into romantic relief. Lantern light began to appear in villa windows adding sparkles of bright reddish-orange color to its soft evening glow. It reminded me of Ma's coral mother of pearl necklace that had been handed down in her family from her great-great grandmother. Ma would sometimes let Elizabeth and I wear the necklace when we were little girls. I remember looking at my reflection in Ma's old cracked mirror with that beautiful, lustrous pearl on its intricate silver chain hanging around my sweaty, dirt-lined neck, its lustrous beauty framed by my plain, drab, usually muddy play clothes. That is the way I thought of San Antonio de Bexar—a beautiful, ornate jewel nestled against the wild, dirty, uncivilized, unsettled Texas countryside.

Danny dropped me off at the tavern and gave me money to rent a room for a couple of days until we figured out what he was supposed to do and what he was going to do with me. Then he went over to the Alamo to report to Colonel Neill. I thought his commander was a captain, but Danny corrected me by explaining that Captain Neill had been promoted to colonel after the battle for San Antonio. The different ranks always confused me, so I usually didn't try to remember someone's rank unless I had to speak to them. I was proud though, because now Danny was a sergeant, which made him an important member of his squad, I think.

I had always been interested in meeting people, and I was amazed at the many different backgrounds of the people I met my first few days in town. Most of the citizens were of Mexican descent. Some were from older, established, wealthy criollo families who had lived in the Mexican territories for generations, and the rest belonged to the peasant working class. Then there were the Anglos who had come to Texas because of the cheap, plentiful land. But there were also a small but significant group of free black people who had come to Texas as slaves, but had either bought or obtained their freedom some other way and now owned land and businesses. The blacksmith in town was a free black man who had come to Texas as a slave. Felipe Elua was a wealthy free black man who owned several houses and a large tract of land. He liked to come by the tavern each morning for a cup of coffee and to visit with the Garcias. Of course, there were also those black people who had been brought to Texas against their will as slaves, but since the Mexican government forbade slavery, I felt sure all black people in Texas would eventually gain their freedom. Anyway, back to our first day in Bexar.

Mr. and Mrs. Juan Garcia owned the tavern. They were a middle-aged couple who had lived in San Antonio all of their lives. Luckily they spoke English, even though it was somewhat broken. They had a room for rent and I paid for a three-night stay. We had brought some of our money, but I could tell it wouldn't last long what with paying room rent and stable rent for the animals. I had no idea when, or if, Danny would get paid, so before I went to unpack the mule that first evening, I asked Mrs. Garcia if she needed any help in the kitchen, cleaning rooms, or serving customers.

"I don't have an experience working in a tavern," I explained, "but I can clean and do some cooking, and I am willing to learn," I added hopefully.

She looked at me doubtfully, but just then a large group of loud Texian soldiers came into the tavern, and her look changed to one of exhausted exasperation. "Okay," she said. "I give you a try." I thanked her, hurriedly unloaded the mule, took him and Buster to the stable down the street, and ran back to start work.

I knew Ma would not approve of my working in that tavern, but it turned out to be quite an educational experience for me. Danny had to report for duty before sunrise every day, so we would go downstairs and eat breakfast with the Garcias, then he would leave to go to the Alamo, and I would help Mrs. Garcia prepare breakfast for any of the hungover soldiers who awoke in time to eat before reporting for duty. I would then go and clean any rooms that had been occupied the night before and come back downstairs to help Mrs. Garcia prepare for dinner. Mrs. Garcia was such a patient, friendly person. She not only taught me how to prepare Mexican dishes, but also to speak Spanish. She and I spoke only Spanish while working together which enabled me to learn the basics of the language pretty quickly.

Many of the men from the Alamo garrison came to the tavern expecting to be served a big midday meal since this was usually the only decent meal they would eat all day. We usually stayed pretty busy until around two, and then business would usually slow down until around five or six in the evening when most of the men got off work and began their nightly drinking. They continued drinking inside the tavern until we closed at ten at night. After that they carried their drinking party out into the streets, where they eventually would either stumble back to their quarters or pass out on the tavern's porch. I found all of that drinking quite appalling, and I was glad Danny didn't drink that heavily, although he did have a few drinks with his buddies at the end of the day.

The only good thing about the drinking was that it caused the men to have very loose tongues, so I heard quite a few interesting stories and learned all the rumors about the Texians' next move against Mexico. It seemed there was a lot of confusion going on in the new Provisional Government. Many in the government wanted to invade Matamoros, Mexico, while we had the advantage of our recent victory over Cos. Many men had left to join up with this group leaving only about 104 men with Colonel Neill to defend San Antonio de Bexar. General Houston and Governor Smith opposed the invasion, and some were threatening to replace General Houston as commander-in-chief and to depose Governor Smith, who refused to step down as governor. It all sounded like a huge, depressing mess. In fact, at one point, after listening to it all, I was tempted to start drinking myself.

It seemed like the only thing that was going right was the fortification work at the Alamo. "Sam, you have to come see what we have done to the Alamo when you get a chance. Colonel Neill is a genius when it comes to implementing the structural reinforcing of walls, building cannon placements, and all the general fortification work. You'll be surprised at the size of the Alamo garrison. We have a brilliant engineer, Green Jameson, assisting us with the structural design work." Danny seemed very excited and passionate about what was going on at the Alamo, and it made me happy to see him that way.

"I was thinking about taking a tour of the town tomorrow after the dinner crowd leaves, so I'll come by," I promised.

The next day, after the dinner crowd had left and while the Garcias were taking a siesta, I set out to explore the town. San Antonio de Bexar was a lovely little town arranged around a central plaza that was shaded by a huge oak tree. Its most striking feature was the San Fernando Cathedral with its bell tower rising majestically above the town, an ornately crafted architectural reminder of the town's origins. The houses of the wealthier residents of San Antonio bordered the plaza. I passed the

Veramendi house, the de la Garza house, and the Navarro house. Mrs. Garcia had told me that their grand adobe walls surrounded a beautiful central courtyard with gardens of flowering shrubs and exotic flowers that stretched down to the San Antonio River. The river itself was lined with cypress trees and cottonwoods that made the sound of falling rain when the breeze stirred their leaves. Since it was winter, the flowers, shrubs, and trees had long ago shed their leaves and flowers, but I could just imagine how beautiful these gardens must look in the spring and summer with azaleas, hibiscus, and magnolia trees in full bloom. Smaller adobe homes lined the other streets that comprised the town proper.

I paused sadly in front of the Veramendi house and wondered if anyone still lived there. I had heard that the Veramendi family had died in the cholera epidemic of 1832. James Bowie, who along with his volunteers had fought at the Battle of San Concepcion, had been married to Ursula Veramendi, the beautiful daughter of Viceroy Juan Veramendi, the man who had built this house. Ursula and their two children had all died in the epidemic. It was such a romantically tragic story, a real-life version of one of Shakespeare's plays.

As I paused outside the door, it suddenly burst open and the figure of a large man filled the doorway. His intense brown eyes were slightly blurred with drink, and he held a bottle of whisky in his hand. My eyes widened in fear as they traveled up from the broad chest to the stern face and steely blue eyes.

"Who are you and what do you want?" he demanded brusquely after taking a swig from the bottle.

I swallowed hard. "I'm Samantha Autry and I was just exploring the town and stopped to admire your home. My husband, Danny Autry, is assigned to Colonel Neill's command," I finished lamely and dropped my gaze.

He must have noticed the fear in my eyes. In a softer tone, he said, "Sorry for my rudeness. My name is Jim Bowie and I was just on my way back to the Alamo. I'm commanding some volunteers there. So...I guess we'll be seeing each other around town."

My jaw dropped and I couldn't manage to say another word. He just grinned at the surprised look on my face, closed the door to the house, and ambled on down the street toward the Alamo, tossing his half-empty whisky bottle to an inebriated soldier sitting by the side of the street.

I couldn't wait to see Danny and tell him who I had met. I ran across the bridge that crossed the San Antonio River and passed the jacales where the poorest citizens of San Antonio lived. I found Danny and several others working on hoisting a cannon to its new, reinforced placement atop the west wall facing town. This was the first time I had really had a chance to see the Alamo.

The Garcias had informed me that its proper name was San Antonio de Valero after its patron saint, Saint Anthony, but was nicknamed the Alamo because of the cottonwood trees that lined the water ditches flowing into its grounds. The Spanish built it as a mission for the purpose of converting the local Indians to Christianity. It contained a rectangular court which covered three acres whose walls housed small adobe rooms. On the eastern side were buildings which had been made into soldier's barracks, a hospital, kitchen, and pens for holding livestock. Its defining feature, the chapel, stood on the southwestern corner, its ornately carved front adorned with the statue of St. Anthony, but, oddly enough, it had no roof. The chapel was unfinished, which seemed strange considering it was founded by missionaries to convert the Indians. I found out later that disease and Indian reluctance to conversion caused it to be abandoned before it was finished. The southern side was an unfinished area of the wall known as the palisade which Mr. Jameson and his men were attempting to shore up with dirt and logs.

As I ran up to the wall, Danny spotted me and came down to greet me. I hadn't seen him in a few days because he had been working so late that he had opted to stay in the Alamo barracks for the last few nights. He gave me a long, passionate kiss right there in front of all those men, which was a little embarrassing, but I really didn't mind.

"You'll never guess who's in town," I announced breathlessly, both from running and from his kiss. "Colonel Bowie and his men! I ran into Colonel Bowie in front of the Veramendi house."

"Yes, I know, my little gossip butterfly," Danny said, laughing. "He and his men arrived here at the Alamo this morning to talk to Colonel Neill. It seems he is to command the volunteers and Colonel Neill is to command the regulars."

"Oh," I said, a little deflated that my news wasn't much news after all. "Well, are you coming to the tavern tonight? I have to work but you could spend the night there, and I promise I'll get you up early so you won't be late for formation."

"I was planning on surprising you and doing that anyway," he teased with a mischievous gleam in his eyes. "I'll see you later."

The next couple of weeks proved to be very hectic with the occurrence of a series of extraordinary events. First, Lt. Col. Travis and his cavalrymen arrived to reinforce the Alamo. Then, to my unbelievably pleasant surprise, Congressman David Crockett arrived with a group of volunteers all from Tennessee. I honestly couldn't believe it! I had heard Pa talk so much about him and here he was in the flesh!

The night he and his men arrived, the tavern soon filled up with hungry, thirsty men ready to celebrate. Even though I was terribly busy serving drinks and food, I don't believe I have ever had so much fun. Colonel Crockett, as he was now called by his men, had brought his fiddle, and began playing all the old dancing songs from my childhood. It was just like being home again! And surprise of all surprises, Danny's Uncle Micajah was with him! He had caught up with Crockett's group in Memphis and traveled with them to Texas. Danny was so excited to see his uncle he could hardly stand it and couldn't wait to introduce me to him. "Samantha, this is Uncle Micajah; Uncle Micajah, my wife Samantha."

"I am so glad to finally meet you, Uncle Micajah," I said, holding out my hand.

"It is definitely a pleasure to meet you, pretty little lady. Danny, I don't know how you managed it, but she is definitely a keeper!" Then he gave me a big hug, grabbed me around the waist, and whirled me off to the dance floor.

After he had finished playing a few songs, one of the men asked Colonel Crockett why he had quit Congress. He told us he had been defeated in his last election because of that scoundrel President Andrew Jackson, and he had told his constituents, "That's okay. You all can go to hell, and I'm going to Texas." Everyone in the tavern cheered and the drinking and dancing resumed. Danny and I sat down with Uncle Micajah and cajoled him into telling us all about how he had come to join up with David Crockett.

"Well," he said. "I had just hit Nacogdoches when I saw this bunch of men going from one saloon to the next drinking and carousing and having a good ol' time. I went up to one of them and asked who they were with."

"Why we're travelin' with David Crockett," they said, "and we're headed to Texas."

"Me too," I told them. "You mind if I join you fellers?"

Just at that moment, Ol' Davy himself walked up. "O'course not," he said, "the more, the merrier!"

"So I joined up with them and here I am," he said, "and mighty pleased and surprised to find you two here also."

We laughed and Danny said, "Us too, Uncle Micajah, us too." Needless to say, we had quite a party that night.

The next day, the town of Bexar received some disappointing news. Colonel Neill had to leave and go home because of sickness in his family, leaving Lt. Colonel Travis, who was the second ranking officer, in charge of the Alamo. This did not sit well with Colonel Bowie or most of the other men who liked Bowie better than Travis. I could understand their position. Lt. Col. Travis always presented a very professional, serious, aloof demeanor to everyone…all of the time. I personally sometimes wondered if he was human. I attributed his attitude to his being only twenty-six years old and in command of men who were five to ten years older. Colonel Bowie, on the other hand, was an older, more experienced officer who drank and caroused with his men as if he was just "one of them." He was definitely the more popular of the two.

Over the next few days, things got pretty tense between the two groups of men, and it all came to a head when Lt. Col. Travis had one of Colonel Bowie's men arrested. I was serving drinks when I saw one of Colonel Bowie's men talking to him. All of a sudden, he jumped up out of his chair, and charged after Lt. Col. Travis.

"Travis, you have no business disciplining my men."

"Bowie, Colonel Neill left me in command of the Alamo, and I will discipline any soldier I see fit."

Colonel Bowie started toward Travis and I thought there was going to be a fight when someone suggested that the men hold a vote to see who would command the Alamo. Colonel Bowie won the vote, but since he was a volunteer, the regulars had to be commanded by a commissioned officer. In order to keep the peace, Bowie and Travis agreed to co-command the Alamo. With the Alamo walls physically rebuilt and reinforced and a number of cannons available, Colonel Bowie and Colonel Travis determined that if and when the Mexicans returned, they must be stopped at San Antonio. The stage was set and all the characters in place for a battle that would define the course of Texas history and inexorably, painfully change my life.

7

February 23 began for me the way all the other days in Bexar had begun. I got up early to help Mrs. Garcia prepare breakfast. Danny had been staying at the Alamo the past few days helping Mr. Jameson finish working on the palisade next to the chapel, and I had made plans to go by there that afternoon after the dinner crowd had left the tavern. My happy mood at the thought of going to see Danny quickly changed to irritation when I noticed all the men passed out on the tables, hungover reminders of the party the night before. I would have to bring them all coffee and try to get them awake and out of the tavern so that we could serve breakfast.

But something was different this morning. I didn't smell coffee brewing or bacon frying. As I looked outside the tavern's swinging front doors, I saw Mexican citizens with loaded wagons heading out of town. Puzzled, I went to the kitchen to find Mrs. Garcia and found her and Mr. Garcia packing some food, their wagon loaded with all of their belongings just outside the door.

"Mrs. Garcia, como esta?" I asked.

"Samantha, we are leaving and you need to come with us. Santa Anna is just outside of town. You must leave, now!"

"What? I have to go find Danny!" I told her. I gave her and Mr. Garcia a quick hug. "Vaya con Dios," I told them and ran out of the door toward the Alamo, my heart beating so hard, it threatened to choke me.

I ran around to the palisade and found Danny working alongside some of Crockett's men. "Danny!" I cried. "Most of the Mexican citizens are leaving town. They say Santa Anna is here!"

"What? Samantha, slow down and tell me what is going on."

I took a deep breath. "Danny, people have packed their belongings and are leaving town. The Garcias are leaving too. Mrs. Garcia told me word is Santa Anna is not far from Bexar."

Just at that moment, the bell in the San Fernando Church tower began to clang. I looked up and saw Daniel Cloud swinging on that bell rope for all he was worth. Lt. Col. Travis emerged from his quarters at a dead run heading for the church tower. I watched him confer with Cloud, then come back down and order Dr. John Sutherland and John Smith to ride out toward the south side of town and see what was going on. Danny and I ran to the top of the west wall to watch for their return. After a while, we heard someone yell "Open the gate," and looked over the wall just in time to see Sutherland and Smith riding back at a full gallop. The look on their faces told us all we needed to know. Santa Anna was here and he had brought his huge army with him.

I ran back to the tavern to collect my belongings and then went to the stables to get Buster and the mule. Someone had taken the mule but luckily Buster was still there looking very nervous. I hurriedly put on his harness and saddle and rode him back to the Alamo.

Chaos reigned within the Alamo's walls. Lt. Colonel Travis ordered everyone left in town to withdraw into the Alamo for protection. Those Tejano families who supported Santa Anna stayed in town, the rest entered the Alamo's protective walls. Most of these were the families of the men defending the fort. There were wagons full of supplies rolling in, and women chasing children who were running around everywhere. The women just managed to get their children corralled before one of the men herded cattle into the cattle pens on the east side. The women were looking pretty harried, so I decided to help get everyone settled after I unsaddled Buster and put him in one of the pens.

After accomplishing as much of this impossible task as I possibly could, I rejoined Danny on the west wall. We just stared, transfixed by what we saw. Hundreds, perhaps thousands, of Mexican soldiers were pouring into San Antonio. I saw a battalion marching down the main street by the plaza playing music (yes, they even brought a band) with Santa Anna in the lead, tipping his large plumed hat to the crowd, who were yelling "Vive Santanna."

I saw him pause before a house where a pretty Mexican girl who looked to be about sixteen was standing in the doorway. He made a point of bowing to her and smiling. I had heard he liked to romance and then pretend to marry young girls in the territories he conquered. I say "pretend" because he supposedly had a wife, although I couldn't understand anyone wanting to marry him unless it was for his position or his fortune. He was just a disgusting person. Yet the sight of all those soldiers was terrifying!

It seemed Santa Anna wasn't finished with his role as the gift giver of terror for the day. Someone shouted, "Look at the tower!" We all looked toward the San Fernando Bell Tower and witnessed six Mexican soldiers raising the flag of "No Quarter" on the top of its beautiful dome. A chill went through me. That meant that Santa Anna would take no prisoners of war. We would win or we would all die.

Lt. Col. Travis didn't seem to be too perturbed by this display. "Fire the eighteen- pounder, boys."

The cannon boomed and a cheer erupted from everyone standing on the west wall. Our elation was short-lived, because, just at that moment, I saw a rider carrying a white flag emerge from the south gate heading toward two Mexican soldiers on horseback. Colonel Bowie had sent out Green B. Jameson under the white flag of parley to meet with Mexican colonels. Lt. Col. Travis was as furious with Bowie for trying to parley with the Mexicans as Santa Anna was furious with the Texians for revolting against his dictatorship. A serious confrontation ensued between the two men.

"Colonel Bowie, what gives you the authority to send Jameson out there to parley with the Mexicans?" yelled Travis.

"Damn it, Travis, I am trying to get us out of this mess. You know we don't stand a chance against that huge army with only 157 men," Colonel Bowie snapped back. Just at that moment, Major Jameson returned with Santa Anna's answer. He handed it to Colonel Bowie.

"It doesn't matter anyway, Travis," Colonel Bowie retorted between clenched teeth. "Santa Anna demands surrender at his discretion, otherwise every man in the Alamo will be put to the sword." He angrily threw the piece of paper to the ground.

Lt. Col. Travis replied, "I've sent dispatches for help to General Houston and the government at San Felipe, to Gonzales, and to Colonel Fannin at Goliad. Help will come in a few days. We just have to hold out until then."

"Well, I hope you're right, Travis, I hope you're right," Colonel Bowie snapped and stomped off angrily.

Just then, the west wall shook beneath my feet as a Mexican cannon fired at the Alamo barely hitting the wall because it hadn't been properly placed, but causing mortar to fly. Both sides began shooting and the crack and whine of rifle shot pierced the air. I stayed by Danny and the other Tennesseans and kept Danny's rifles loaded. Colonel Crockett actually managed to kill one Mexican soldier. After a while, the Mexican firing ceased as suddenly as it had begun. It seemed Santa Anna had decided to call it a day, so we began cooking supper.

After supper, I climbed to the top of the west wall again to see what the Mexicans were doing. Cook fires were burning across the field where the Mexicans were camped and I could hear talking and laughing. They seemed mighty confident and, as far as I could tell, they had every reason to feel that way. Inside the Alamo, everyone was pretty physically and emotionally exhausted by the events of the day and things became pretty quiet.

We soon learned Santa Anna's surprises didn't end when the sun went down. At about ten, just as everyone was drifting off to sleep, the Mexicans began to play a haunting melody. I saw Lt. Col. Travis and Colonel Bowie walk up to the west wall, and of course, I followed because I had to know what was going on. Colonel Crockett and Danny joined us.

"What's that song?" asked Colonel Crockett.

"The Deguello," answered Travis. "It means 'slit throat.'" As soon as he said this, the Mexicans began to fire their cannon. We quickly got off the wall and ran for cover.

That night the Mexican's continuous shelling seemed to last forever. But dawn eventually arrived, and with it, a short lull in the constant pounding of the cannon. I had spent the night with Danny at his post at the far northwest corner of the wall mainly because I was afraid, and he was the only one who could make me feel safe. I slowly got up from my cramped position against the corner of the wall, stretched my sore back, and went to help the women cook breakfast.

I had met Mrs. Dickinson, Almeron Dickinson's wife, and Mrs. Esparza, Enrique Esparza's wife, while working at the tavern. There was also Betty, Colonel Bowie's cook and a few other slaves who accompanied their masters into the Alamo. Betty was a great cook, and during the siege, she taught me a lot of different ways to cook corn and potatoes, which was about all we had except for beef. After breakfast, I became bored sitting in the chapel with the women, so I went out to find Danny.

I found him with Colonel Bowie and some other men attempting to mount a twelve-pound cannon on the west wall. I noticed that Colonel Bowie had been coughing a lot lately, and as he pushed against one of the wheel's spokes to roll the cannon up the scaffold, he began to cough violently and let go of the wheel. I heard several of the men yell, "Look out below!" as the big cannon began to roll backward and Danny and the other men jumped out of the way. I watched in horror as it rolled to the edge of the scaffold taking Colonel Bowie with it. The cannon reached the edge and stopped rolling, but Colonel Bowie fell off the scaffold. The fall broke several of his ribs. He would never fully recover, because his injuries aggravated his illness, which I found out later, was typhoid pneumonia. Lt. Col. Travis was now in full command.

Danny didn't want me around the cannon placements, so I helped Mr. Jamison shore up some damaged places in the west wall with logs and bags of dirt. It was heavy work and I knew I probably wasn't a lot of help. But there were only 157 men to fight off all those Mexicans and try to keep the old fort's walls from falling down from all the shelling, so I figured the men needed all the help they could get. As I was finishing up helping to fill a hole with bags of dirt, Colonel Crockett called me to come up on the wall.

"Come here, Samantha, I want you to see something."

Curious and, I had to admit, tired of moving bags of dirt, I climbed up onto the west wall beside him. The sight of all those Mexican soldiers and their artillery made my knees feel weak. I noticed the Mexican cannon fire had slowed down some and now I could see why. During the night, the Mexicans had placed a cannon battery closer to the Alamo's walls. Unfortunately for them, Colonel Crockett and his men were picking them off like turkeys at a turkey shoot with their deadly accurate long rifles.

"Samantha, you want to get a look at Ol' Santy Anny?'

"Sure! Which one is he?" It was hard to distinguish one Mexican from the other, there were so many of them moving around down there.

Juan Seguin who was standing by Colonel Crockett, pointed just to my right near one of the jacales. "He is the one with the big plumed hat, gold embroidered uniform, and the gold braid epaulettes." I could see him giving orders to one of the Mexican artillerymen about to fire one of the newly placed cannon.

"Watch this, Samantha," said Colonel Crockett. Before Santa Anna could order the artillerymen to fire their cannon, Colonel Crockett grabbed his extra rifle and shot one of them dead. This really enraged the Mexican general, and I heard him along with several other officers shout, "Fuego!" A barrage of cannon fire erupted and we quickly ducked down behind the wall. I covered my ears as the cannon balls hit the wall and exploded. My ears were ringing and my heart was pounding with fear, but I couldn't help grinning when I saw the look of sly satisfaction that crossed Colonel Crockett's face.

After the barrage of cannon fire ended, I heard a commanding voice shout, "Mrs. Autry, I need you to come down from that wall and report to me immediately."

Oh no…it was Lt. Col. Travis. And I could tell by the added severity in his autocratic tone that I was probably in trouble.

I climbed down from the wall and approached him cautiously. "Yes, sir?" I asked hesitantly.

"Mrs. Autry, what were you doing up there on that wall?" he demanded.

"Colonel Crockett and Uncle Micajah wanted me to see Santa Anna, sir."

He gave me a stern look and seemed about to reproach me for my actions, but changed his mind. Instead he said, "I noticed you have been assisting the men with patching the walls. That is not women's work, and I think you should be with the women."

"I know, sir, but between meals, the women are just trying to keep themselves and their children calm, and frankly, sir, screaming children get on my nerves. So I thought since you are so short-handed, I could be more useful helping the men as much as I can…sir." I was too intimidated to meet his steady gaze and just stared at the ground.

I heard him sigh irritably. "Very well, Mrs. Autry, I have a job for you. I need you to find Albert Martin and bring him to me immediately. I have a message that must go to Gonzales, then to San Felipe de Austin as soon as possible."

I found Mr. Martin helping with a cannon placement and told him Lt. Col. Travis needed to see him. I walked back with him to the colonel's quarters and while he was getting his instructions, I happened to glance down and see the letter that Lt. Col. Travis wanted him to deliver. It was a letter I would not and could not ever forget as long as I lived. It was both patriotic and imploring, and seemed to compel immediate action with its stirring language:

> TO THE PEOPLE OF TEXAS AND ALL AMERICANS IN THE WORLD—Fellow citizens and compatriots. I am besieged by a thousand or more of the Mexicans under Santa Anna. I have sustained a continual bombardment and cannonade for 24 hours and have not lost a man. The enemy has demanded a surrender at discretion, otherwise the garrison are to be put to the sword if the fort is taken. I have answered the demand with a cannon shot, and our flag still waves proudly from the walls. I shall never surrender or retreat. Then I call on you in the name of Liberty, of patriotism, and everything dear to the American character, to come to our aid with all dispatch. The enemy is receiving reinforcement daily and will no doubt increase to three or four thousand in four or five days. If this call is neglected, I am determined to sustain myself as long as possible and die like a soldier who never forgets what is due to his own honor and that of his country. VICTORY OR DEATH. (Tinkle, 1958, pg. 75)

My heart sank even as the words became seared in my brain. For the first time, I finally realized that we might all die.

8

Lt. Col. Travis gave the letter to Martin along with his instructions, and then turned back to me. I frantically searched his resolute, stern expression for some reassurance that reinforcements would come, that we would be all right. All I heard from the men, especially Colonel Crockett and Uncle Micajah, was that General Houston and Colonel Fannin from Goliad would be here as soon as they heard about our plight. In fact, they felt sure both men were on their way here already. Now after reading that letter and seeing the look in Lt. Col. Travis's eyes, I wasn't so sure.

"Colonel Travis? Reinforcements will come, won't they?" I asked anxiously. I had noticed that most of the men called him Colonel Travis even though his true rank was lieutenant colonel, so in order to simplify all this military rank business, I decided to just call him Colonel Travis also.

"I believe they will. I hope they will," he said hesitantly, running his fingers through his fiery red hair and pacing the room. Suddenly he stopped, looked straight at me and said, "God knows I have sent plenty of messages to Gonzales, Goliad, San Felipe de Austin, and the United States. They will come, I feel confident that they will come."

Even after those last words, I couldn't shake my feelings of doubt and foreboding. "Sir, I thought General Houston and Colonel Fannin are on their way here now."

Colonel Travis sighed heavily. "Mrs. Autry, General Houston sent me here to blow up the Alamo. Colonel Bowie was also ordered to blow it up. The general thinks that the Alamo is a death trap that cannot be defended against Santa Anna's army. But Colonel Bowie and I think that if we don't stop the Mexicans here, or at least deal them a crippling blow, Texas is doomed."

I just stared at him, my mind racing like a cornered rabbit. Finally I said, "Well, sir, our decision has been made, and we will just have to do the best we can to hold off Santa Anna until reinforcements arrive." I realized that I sounded a lot more confident than I felt, and Colonel Travis smiled at my feigned bravado. His smile quickly turned into a frown as the Mexican cannons began to fire again.

The evening of the second day finally arrived with an unusual interlude of silence. I figured the Mexicans had gotten hungry and were taking a break for supper. Some of the men had slaughtered one of the cows that day, and so we had fresh beef that night to go along with our beans, potatoes, and cornbread. The savory, smoky smell of roasting meat improved everyone's mood, and Colonel Crockett even played his fiddle which succeeded in lifting everyone's spirits. The Mexicans still hadn't started firing their cannons again, and we began to hope that maybe they were going to rest that night and let us sleep. Of course we were soon disappointed. At around ten, our spirits sank as we heard a Mexican officer yell "Fuego," shattering our peaceful night with the booming of cannon and fiery streaks of flying cannonballs. It was going to be another very long night.

By the morning of the third day, February 25, we were so exhausted from lack of sleep; we were hoping just to get a nap or two between artillery attacks. But Santa Anna had other plans. As I joined Danny and Uncle Micajah on the west wall, the first thing we noticed was that more Mexican soldiers were marching into Bexar: Santa Anna was receiving reinforcements. Suddenly a Mexican battalion began rolling a battery of cannons right across from the Alamo's front gate and another battalion began gathering along the river as if they were preparing to cross and attack. Alarmed, Colonel Travis noticed that if the Mexicans did cross the river, they would have good cover in the jacales that stood just outside the Alamo walls.

"Men," he yelled, "I need some volunteers to go out and burn down those jacales." By this time, the Mexicans had begun to fire the cannons and were positioned to shoot at anyone or anything that emerged from the Alamo. Despite the evident danger, just about every man, including Danny, volunteered to go. Colonel Travis chose two young men, Charles Despalier and Robert Brown for the job.

Colonel Crockett and his men including Danny loaded their rifles and stood ready, along with Captain Dickinson and his eight pound cannon to provide fire cover for Despalier and Brown. Danny ordered me to go down and shelter with the women, but of course, I wouldn't go. I told him I was going to stay and help reload rifles, and he could divorce me later if he didn't like it. He gave me a withering look and handed me his powder and shot. I accepted them without a word and smiled smugly to myself when he wasn't looking. I glanced at Colonel Crockett and noticed that, unfortunately, he had witnessed our little scene. My smile disappeared from my face until I noticed the admiring grin on his face. I smiled back at him; then turned to face the action.

It wasn't long before the Mexicans started crossing the bridge that spanned the San Antonio River and led to the Alamo. Although there were probably only about three hundred soldados, it looked as if there were more than one thousand of them all coming at us at once! All the men lining the west wall began to fire. Mexican sodados began to crumple to the ground as Colonel Crockett's Tennessee sharpshooters hit their marks. Captain Dickinson's cannon roared, spewing lethal amounts of grape and canister shot, and my pulse quickened with excitement at the noise of the battle. I was standing alongside the best riflemen in

Texas, and I was fighting with my Danny. My hands were steady as I reloaded Danny's two rifles and handed them back to him. I was not afraid.

I couldn't say the same for those Mexicans. They were scattering for cover inside those jacales like scared chickens. We fought off those Mexicans for two hours until they finally gave up and retreated back across the river dragging their dead and wounded with them. Just at that moment, first one, then another, and another of those jacales began to smoke and burst into flames. Thank the Lord, Despallier and Brown had survived and had managed to accomplish their mission. I leaned over the wall just in time to see them running like the devil through the main gate to safety.

We all descended from the wall into the courtyard with the men cheering and slapping each other on the back. Even though he was still angry with me, Danny gave me a huge kiss. We had won the first major skirmish against Santa Anna's "professional army." Even while I did my share of basking in the glow of victory, an ominous dark cloud began to creep across that glow; for I had noticed the new artillery batteries the Mexicans had managed to erect before the skirmish began and the continuing stream of Mexican reinforcements.

I did my best to avoid Danny the rest of the day because I didn't want to hear his lecture. I loved Danny with all my heart, but there were times when he was just entirely too bossy. As I made my way past the hospital quarters, I saw one of the doors standing ajar and heard someone call my name in a hoarse voice. It was Colonel Bowie.

Now I had to admit, if Colonel Travis intimidated me, the sight of Colonel Bowie actually put the fear of God in me. I had heard of his reputation as a fighter and adventurer, but had never realized how physically imposing he was until that day I ran into him at the Veramendi house. Reluctantly I entered the sick room. Two Mexican women were tending to him, and I got the impression that one of them might be related to him from the way they were speaking to each other.

"What can I do for you, sir?" I asked.

"Come sit down in this chair over here and talk to me. I heard from our stiff-necked commander that you insisted on participating in that little altercation with the Mexicans this morning."

"Yes, sir. I guess I'm on everyone's bad side right now. Danny's mad at me too. That's why I'm on this side of the fort…trying to avoid him. To be honest, sir, I'm tired and not in any mood for a lecture." I couldn't believe I had made that last statement, and my eyes widened in apprehension at the thought of the reprimand I figured was about to follow.

He must have noticed the look on my face because he grinned and said, "I wasn't planning on lecturing you. I wanted to hear your version of how our first little skirmish with Santa Anna turned out. The account Colonel Travis gave to me sounded like a military dispatch…very boring."

So I told him all the details of the battle. How the Mexican soldiers had tried to cross the river and how they didn't even come close to succeeding due to our superior marksmanship. I also told him about Despallier and Brown's bravery in burning down the jacales under heavy Mexican fire. He looked both pleased at my news and a little disappointed. I figured his disappointment was due to the fact that he had missed all the action.

"Don't worry, sir," I told him, trying to sound as optimistic as possible, "you'll get in on the next fight."

"I don't think so, Mrs. Autry. In fact, I don't believe I'm going to be of much use from now on. You see, I'm pretty sure I'm dying."

I didn't know what to say to this, and I guess he could tell by the look on my face that I felt sorry for him because that mischievous grin returned to his face as he added, "Also, don't count on our illustrious lieutenant colonel letting you get by without a lecture. Neither will your husband if he is worth his salt as a man, and I have heard he is a very brave man."

"Yes, sir, he is," I answered proudly.

"You know, Mrs. Autry, you remind me a lot of my deceased wife, Ursula. She had a lot of spirit also. I found it pretty much impossible to change her mind once she had made it up about something." Suddenly he began to cough and I noticed spots of blood on the handkerchief he used to cover his mouth. One of the women hurried over with some sort of drink which seemed to calm the cough. "Here is a picture of her." He pulled a small framed picture from the pocket of a saddlebag near his cot and handed it to me.

"Please call me Samantha, sir," I said as I took the frame. It was a picture of one of the most beautiful women I had ever seen. Her thick black hair was piled on top of her head under the customary lace hair piece worn by the aristocratic Spanish women. Her delicate features were accentuated by beautiful dark eyes and the half smile that played across her full lips.

"Sir, she is beautiful!" I whispered in awe and then realized that she, along with his two children, had died in the cholera epidemic that had swept through Mexico. I glanced at the colonel and noticed his eyes welling up with tears as he stared at her picture. Seeing this made me realize how much he missed her and what a beautiful, happy life they must have shared together.

"I thought I was keeping them safe when I sent them with my father-in-law to Monclova," he half whispered to himself. "I never thought cholera would reach there." I had heard of Monclova. It was a resort town located somewhere in the mountains of Mexico.

I didn't know what to say that could possibly be of much comfort, so we sat in silence for a little while. Finally, I asked, "Sir, if Bexar brings back so many painful memories, why did you come back?"

"I guess because to me Bexar will always be home. The time I spent married to Ursula were probably the best days of my life. Up until then, I had pretty much been a no-good scoundrel. My brother and I smuggled slaves into the United States, we swindled land in Arkansas, and I was always getting into knife fights and duels. I just didn't care what I did or who I hurt as long as I was making money or accumulating land. But then I met Ursula here in Bexar, and somehow she made me want to be a better person just so I could be worthy of her company. For some unknown reason, she fell in love with me, and for the first time in my life, I was the happiest man alive. I went into business with her father, the Viceroy here in town, running a cotton textile mill in Saltillo, Mexico, and buying property in the United States. When that cholera epidemic struck, I sent them to Montclova where my father-in-law had a summer home. I just knew they would be safe there while I finished some business deals. But I was wrong." With these last words, his voice broke and he cleared his throat and looked away.

Suddenly, I had an idea. "I'll be right back, sir," I told him and went to find Uncle Micajah. "Uncle Micajah, I need to borrow a bottle of your moonshine." I grabbed one of the bottles he had squirreled away inside his mule pack before he had time to object, and took it back to Colonel Bowie's room. I found two cups on the table next to his bed and poured us half a cup each. I was so very happy Ma could not see what I was about to do because she would have killed me.

"Sir," I said. "I know everyone always tells you how sorry they are about what happened to your family. So instead, I would like to propose a toast." I held up my cup and said, "To your beautiful wife and family and the wonderful life you were blessed to enjoy with them." We drained our cups and I managed not to choke even though the liquor burned my throat and my eyes began to water.

After that first drink, Colonel Bowie told me stories about his youth and fighting with his brother Rezin, and scrapes he and his buddies had gotten into over the years. I couldn't help but laugh at some of the outrageous situations he described. After our second drink, he told stories about his time wrestling alligators. He explained, "You see, I would get on the gator's back and basically ride it holding its mouth shut until the animal passed out with exhaustion. Then my friends, thinking the animal was dead, would creep up close to it to check it out. After a few seconds, that gator would spring to life thrashing and snapping its jaws! My brave compadres would run so fast gettin' out of that bayou that the snakes couldn't keep up."

By this time I was laughing so hard my stomach hurt and tears blinded my eyes. The more I laughed, the more outrageous his stories became and the more he laughed. I got kind of worried because laughing made him cough, but he seemed to be enjoying himself too much to quit. Finally he said, "You know, Mrs. Autry, Samantha, you are quite a lady."

We had just poured our third drink, when uninvited visitors ruined our party. "Mrs. Autry, I wish to speak with you outside." I looked up to see Colonel Travis silhouetted in the doorway. By this time I had started to feel a strange lightheaded sensation, which was closely followed by the realization that I didn't really care what that stiff-necked, self-righteous lieutenant colonel thought. In fact, he positively annoyed me with his strict adherence to rules and regulations, especially since I wasn't even a soldier in his stupid old army anyway. I rolled my eyes at Colonel Bowie, who laughed as I walked rather unsteadily outside. Danny was waiting there also along with Uncle Autry who had blabbed about my whiskey confiscation. Also Colonel Crockett and Juan Seguin, who just happened to be passing by, stopped to join the little lynch mob. So, they were going to gang up on me, were they? Well, let them go ahead and try. After that second drink, I really didn't care. I had never had strong drink before and it was making me pretty belligerent.

"Gentlemen," I began. "I realize I have offended your protective male sensibilities by endeavoring to be of assistance during this morning's little…adventure. I feel I accomplished my objective and am not one whit sorry for doing so. But if it will make you all feel better, I will do my best to adhere to your wishes and endeavor to keep to my role as a helpless female. Now if you will excuse me, I need to go help prepare dinner." With that said, I turned and began walking rather unsteadily toward the cooking area. I heard Danny and Colonel Travis say some very ungentlemanly words while Juan and Colonel Crockett laughed out loud.

When I reached the kitchen area, Betty took one look at me and asked, "Girl, have you been drinking?"

Knowing it would be useless to deny the fact, I replied, "Yes, ma'am, it's my first time, and I'm really starting to regret it."

Betty laughed and said, "Well, you just sit over here in this corner and eat you some bread…and stay away from the knives and the fire until you sober up."

Eating some food helped to clear my head of that fuzzy feeling, but then it started to hurt and my stomach began to feel slightly queasy. Although I felt good about making Colonel Bowie feel better, I decided then that drinking liquor was not for me. I finished helping Betty prepare dinner, took two plates and went to find Danny at his post on the west wall. He didn't say anything. He just gave me a reproachful look, took his plate, and began to eat. After dinner, we sat on the wall with me leaning back in his arms and watched the Mexican camp below.

That night a bitterly cold norther blew in, making things more miserable than usual. With only 157 men to man the fort, there were not enough men to rotate guard positions, so the men had to get what little sleep they could at their posts. I had spent every night with Danny at his post; both of us huddled under the single blanket I had thought to bring. I wished I had thought to bring a few more. I kept expecting my lecture, but it never came. I guess Danny figured we shouldn't spend our time fighting because we might not have much time left. We all were beginning to doubt that help would come.

For the next two days, the Mexican soldados continued their cannon fire every night and to move their artillery ever closer under the cover of darkness to avoid our rifles. They were also getting more reinforcements. We knew it wouldn't be long before the Alamo was completely surrounded and reinforcements would be unable to reach us. It looked more and more as if our doubts about getting any help were doomed to become reality.

By February 27, the fifth day of the siege, we all began to feel desperate. We did have a little excitement that day which helped to take our minds off our situation. Not realizing that we had a well inside the Alamo, the Mexicans decided to try to cut off our water supply by damming the river with logs.

I was helping Sam and Joe, Lt. Col. Travis's and Colonel Bowie's slaves, move bags of dirt and logs to reinforce the palisade nearest the chapel when I heard rifle fire break out atop the west wall and the Mexican cannons begin an all-out ear-splitting barrage mercilessly pounding holes in the Alamo walls. Sam, Joe, and I ran to the wall to find out what was going on. Sam decided to stay at the bottom while Joe and I ran up the ramp to get a better look. Uncle Micajah and two other Tennesseans fired their deadly long guns simultaneously, adding a sharp cracking accompaniment to the shrieking, booming song of Mexican cannon fire. Through the heavy smoke created by the firing weapons, we could just make out seven Mexican soldados trying to drag their dead comrades back to their camp. Suddenly the crack of our rifles firing once again split the air and two more soldados fell to the ground. Once again, Texan marksmanship had saved the day.

Even though we had another small victory to celebrate, a larger cloud loomed over our heads, further dampening our spirits. Santa Anna had totally blocked the road to Gonzales and was closely watching the road to Goliad. Getting help from the outside was becoming increasingly more difficult. That evening, an increasingly desperate Lt. Col. Travis sent James Bonham to Goliad to find out why Fannin had not arrived to relieve the Alamo.

That night after supper, I walked over to the fire where Juan Seguin and his fellow Tejanos were molding rifle balls and cleaning their rifles. Juan and his compadres looked to be in their twenties, their dark good looks reflecting their Mexican heritage. The look of wariness in their eyes made me feel somewhat intimidated, but I liked Juan and I wanted to meet his friends. After all, we were fighting on the same side. I figured we should at least know each other's names. Besides, I was curious as to why they would fight for the Texan cause against their fellow Mexicans.

"Buenos noches," I said and sat down on a log by their fire. They looked up briefly, returned my greeting, and went back to cleaning their rifles. Not a very talkative lot, I thought to myself. After a few moments of silence I said, "Mind if I ask you amigos a question?"

"Depends on the question," answered Juan. I deduced from their cool reception they didn't approve of my working alongside Danny and the others instead of staying with the women, and didn't know exactly how to react to me. I had learned from observing the Garcias and other Mexican families that Mexican women were a little more obedient than me.

"I don't understand," I began. "Why do you fight with us against your own people?"

Juan just stared into the fire a little while before he finally answered, "Mrs. Autry, have your ever heard the saying 'the enemy of my enemy is my friend'?"

"Yes," I answered. "And please, call me Samantha."

"Well, although my brothers on the other side of that wall do not realize it, Santa Anna is the enemy of Mexico's freedom and independence. My family has lived in Coahuilla y Tejas for many generations. When Santa Anna helped Mexico win her independence from Spain, we were very glad because we just knew that now Mexico would be a republic and her people would be free. But we were wrong. Once Santa Anna was elected president, he threw out our republican constitution and made himself dictator of all Mexico. The state of Zacatecas rebelled against Santa Anna's tyranny and paid a heavy price. He killed all of the rebels there who opposed him and then let his army rape and pillage the rest of the population. Before it was over two thousand civilians were killed along with the rebels. Santa Anna killed many of my people and I will have my revenge."

"But don't you all have friends or family fighting with Santa Anna now?"

"Yes, most of these men have family fighting for Santa Anna."

"That must be hard," I said sympathetically. I couldn't help admiring these men. They were willing to fight against their own families for the cause of freedom. "Don't they realize, Santa Anna is a murderous tyrant?"

"I believe they do. But they are afraid of what he will do to them and their families in Mexico if they don't fight for him."

"But don't they realize he will probably do whatever he wants to them anyway? That is what dictators do, you know, because they really don't care about their people."

Juan just shrugged and went back to staring into the fire. Just then, Colonel Travis emerged out of the darkness and into the circle of firelight. "Captain Seguin, I need to speak to you and Mr. Arocha immediately."

"Yes, sir." Juan and Antonio rose to follow the colonel back to his quarters. I bade the rest of the men 'Buenos noches' and wondered back toward the west wall to find Danny.

As I was walking by the barracks, I heard a commotion near the cattle pens. I heard Colonel Travis call for two horses to be saddled right away. I saw the colonel, Juan, and Antonio headed for the corral and I hurried over to see what was going on. Colonel Travis ordered Juan to ride to Gonzales to get help and then to go to the provisional government at Washington-on-the-Brazos to demand more. I gave Juan a concerned look as I helped him saddle up Buster knowing that all the roads out of Bexar were either blocked or being watched by the Mexican Army. It seemed me managing to get Buster into the fort on the first day proved to be very fortuitous. I felt somewhat reassured knowing Juan would be riding Buster because I knew Buster was a fast runner.

"Don't worry, Samantha." Juan smiled at me reassuringly. "We are Mexican and speak Spanish, remember? We'll be able to get through."

"Vaya con Dios, mi amigos," I said, looking anxiously up at him. "Please God, go with them," I repeated softly to myself.

9

The next two days seemed endless and depressing. No reinforcements arrived and none of the messengers Colonel Travis had sent out returned with any word…from anyone. We felt as if we were the only ones left in the whole world…left to face El Diablo himself. And El Diablo continued to rain down fire and brimstone on the Alamo. When we were busy with repairs, cooking, or other chores, the persistent cannonade just seemed to be a huge annoyance that made you jump whenever a cannon shot got close, but otherwise could be tolerated and somewhat ignored. But at night when we were exhausted, it grated on my nerves so badly that I wanted to jump over the wall and run away screaming. That's when Danny would hold me, and we would talk about future plans and improvements we hoped to make on our new home when this nightmare was over.

"I can't wait until Ma and Pa see our place, Danny. Maybe we can add on two more rooms for guests and the whole family can come and stay with us. Your family could come too. We could just have a big family reunion! Then maybe they would all move to Texas and live right next door. Wouldn't that be great?"

Danny gave me a dubious, irritated look and said, "You're not serious, are you?" I just laughed and he gave me a deep, tender kiss which sent shivers all over me. We would usually talk a little more and finally drift off into a fitful, often interrupted sleep until dawn broke.

But on February 29, something happened that made things a little better. I was standing on the south wall with Danny and other Tennesseans that evening, when we saw quite a few riders appear on the Gonzales Road. How they had gotten through Santa Anna's guard, I had no idea, but they were a very welcome sight. I heard someone yell, "Open the gate," and we ran down to see who had come to our rescue.

Suddenly, one of the riders jumped off his horse, grabbed me around the waist, and swung me off the ground in a big hug. It was William! The riders were from Gonzales! I gave him a huge kiss on his cheek, tears of joy and relief flooding my eyes. Danny came up behind and clapped him heartily on the back.

"Welcome brother, welcome," he managed to choke out around the lump in his throat.

I was never so happy to see a group of men in my whole life, and I knew everyone else in the Alamo felt the same. Yet I had never also felt so proud and sad. For there were only thirty-two of them, and they must have known that if more reinforcements did not arrive, they had most likely entered a death trap. But the rest of us figured that if the men from Gonzales got through Santa Anna's lines, then others, hopefully Fannin and his men from Goliad, must be on their way. Though they didn't tell us, the men from Gonzales knew that Fannin was not coming…deathtrap it was.

That night we celebrated like never before. Colonel Crockett played his fiddle and we roasted beef, made cornbread, and cooked the last of the potatoes. Colonel Travis also ordered the gunners to fire two shots into Military Plaza near Bexar's town square to let Santa Anna know that we were still ready for a fight. It would be the last celebration the men at the Alamo would ever experience.

The next day, March 1, dawned clear and cold. After breakfast, Danny and I went up on the west wall to see what Santa Anna had been up to during the night, besides making our lives miserable with shelling. When we got to the top of the wall, I wished I hadn't come to look. More Mexican reinforcements were pouring into Bexar and the Mexican army had us totally surrounded. It would take a large group of reinforcements to get through their forces, and, even then, it would be virtually an impossible task.

That evening after supper, I saw Colonel Crockett leaning against the palisade, cleaning his rifle. I walked over and sat down across from him, hugging my knees to my chest to keep warm and just admiring "Ol Betsy," the rifle his constituents had given him back in Tennessee.

"Samantha, girl, You doin' okay?"

"Yes, sir," I answered, continuing to admire his rifle. "How about yourself?"

"All right, I reckon," he replied. After a few minutes, he asked, "What part of Tennessee are you and Danny from?"

"Danny and I came here from a small settlement on the Nolichucky, not far from Greeneville."

"Really, well, I'll be jiggered! I was born on the Nolichucky and lived there when I was a little boy."

"I know. My pa always talked about you and how proud everybody was that you came from our neck of the woods."

He just grinned a little bashfully and said, "Well, I don't know about that. Most folks in Tennessee don't seem too proud of me now."

I didn't reply to that. Finally, I asked, "Colonel Crockett, do you regret coming to Texas and ending up stuck here in the Alamo?"

"I reckon I do sometimes," he answered. "But then I never could pass up a good fight. My pa was in the volunteer militia that beat the British at the Battle of King's Mountain in North Carolina during the Revolutionary War. He always liked to tell us how they sent those Redcoats a scurryin' off like scared jackrabbits." Colonel Crockett and I both laughed at that thought. "And I fought the Redstick Indians during the War of 1812 when the British tried to use the Indians to help them win the war because they didn't have the gumption to do it on their own. So I figured me and my boys could come down here and lend you all a hand in gittin' rid of Ol' Santy Anny."

We sat quietly for a few minutes staring into the fire. Then I asked, "Do you have family back in Tennessee?"

"Yep, I do. My second wife, Elizabeth is there with our kids keeping things going on the farm. I'm hopin' after this little scrape with Santy Anny is over, she'll be agreeable to comin' to Texas. I don't know, though. I don't think I've been a very good husband what with all my politickin' and tryin' to deal with them polecats in Washington, DC," he said, grinning mischievously.

I smiled and sat quietly for a moment, picturing the colonel with his coonskin cap arguing with those stiff-necked, pompous congressmen in their fancy clothes about bills and such. "If you don't mind my asking, what really happened up there in Washington, DC? I know my pa really liked and respected you and your service there."

"The truth is, I didn't ever get along with President Jackson and his cronies. But I think the straw that broke the mule's back with his bunch was the fact that I just couldn't bring myself to vote for Ol' Andy's Indian Removal Bill. He wanted to move the peaceful Indians in the Southeast to west of the Mississip. I just thought this was wrong. After that nobody would vote for any bills I proposed for my folks, and eventually this lost me my House seat. But that was okay, because I've always figured the most important thing a man can have is a clear conscience. So I have always followed one rule—be sure you're right, then go ahead."

I was struck by the sheer simplicity of this powerful truth. It was a piece of unforgettable wisdom from a most unforgettable man.

We sat in companionable silence for a while longer as he finished cleaning his rifle. Then I asked, "What happened to your first wife?"

He set his rifle aside as a sad, wistful expression replaced his infectious smile. "My Polly died in 1815 of some kind of stomach sickness while we were living in Kentuck. Once the sickness came on her, she didn't last very long. Don't get me wrong, I have feelin's for Elizabeth, but Polly was the love of my life. I surely was sad when she passed on. Ours was kind of a rocky romance to start with. Her ma didn't approve of me at all. But I was determined to marry my Polly and she was determined to marry me, so her ma finally gave in and accepted me into the family."

"I can relate to that," I said, smiling. "Danny and I had to run away because my parents didn't want me to marry him and come to Texas."

"Don't you worry your pretty little head," he said, as his smile returned. "You'll see your folks agin. We're going to give ol' Santa Anna a lickin' he'll never forget." He laughed out loud and went back to making shot for his rifle. But, even though I didn't ask him, I wondered if he really believed this.

Over the next two days, we tried to keep our spirits up by clinging to the hope that reinforcements would come. But nobody else came, and I began to feel depressed and anxious. I went about my duties helping with the cooking, helping the men shore up weak sections of the wall, or working with Joe and Sam to stuff bags of dirt into holes created by Santa Anna's shelling. I asked Joe and Sam if they had given any thought to what would happen if Santa Anna's forces overtook the Alamo.

Sam replied, "Well, Miss Samantha, the Mexicans don't believe in slavery. I hope they just turn us loose like I'm sure they'll do the women and children. At least that's what Ol' John, the blacksmith from town, seems to think."

"Is he here?" I asked, surprised. I hadn't even realized that he had taken refuge in the Alamo along with the rest of us.

"Oh, yes, ma'am, he's been stayin' mostly back at the corral takin' care of the horses."

Joe had been looking thoughtful for a few minutes. Finally, he said, "I plan on fightin' alongside Colonel Travis 'til the end and if I'm still alive, I hope they'll turn me loose."

I stuffed dirt into another bag, then said, "I hate to admit it, but that is one thing on which I agree with Santa Anna. I don't believe in slavery and neither my family nor Danny's family ever owned slaves. I sincerely hope things work out for you boys."

"What are you plannin' to do, Miss Samantha?" asked Sam.

"I plan on fighting alongside Danny until the end," I said, looking up at Sam intently. He just looked at me sadly and nodded and we went back to work.

Later that morning, I checked in on Colonel Bowie, but he was sleeping. I just poked my head in for a moment and asked the two women tending him about his condition. They told me his fever had returned and that he slept most of the time. I thanked them and left.

The next day, March 3, at 11:00 a.m., Jim Bonham returned from Goliad riding the gauntlet of Mexican fire and just making it through the gate. I remember these details vividly for it signaled the beginning of the tragic end that would soon befall us all. I happened to be standing near the gate with Danny when he came through, and we both saw the grim look on his face as he headed straight for Colonel Travis's quarters. Every man who saw Bonham's face knew his news was not good. Then to add insult to injury, we heard loud cheering in Military Plaza. We ran up the ramp to the top of the wall and looked down to see what was going on.

"Oh my God," I heard Danny mutter. I just stood rooted to the wall unable to move or speak as my heart sank to the soles of my feet. Fifteen hundred more Mexican soldados had just arrived in Bexar. This brought the total number of Santa Anna's army to almost five thousand men! I knew it would not be long before Santa Anna launched a full attack on the Alamo. Unless we received a miracle in the form of massive reinforcements within the next day or two, we were doomed.

We had been right about the news James Bonham brought back from Goliad. Colonel Fannin seemed convinced that Goliad was the key to defending Texas, and the Alamo was a lost cause. Fannin tried to talk Bonham into staying at Goliad, but Bonham refused saying his orders were to report back to Travis with his decision. Colonel Travis was furious. I could hear him clear across the Alamo grounds, ranting and raving.

"Santa Anna's main force is here! Fannin could have been here days ago and with his four hundred men, our combined forces would have had a chance to stop him! But no, he wants to keep our forces split so Santa Anna can annihilate us both! God! What an idiot!"

There would be one last letter to leave the Alamo from Colonel Travis, one final plea for help. It would go unanswered. Our fate was sealed.

That night, as Danny and I sat huddled together on the west wall, I began to experience a moment of sheer panic. I just wanted to jump over the side of that wall and run. "Danny," I whispered, "let's run, now."

"Samantha, what are you talking about?"

"Danny, I want to leave! I don't want to die and I don't want *you* to die!"

"Samantha, calm down. We're going to get out of this mess. Reinforcements could still get here in time. Houston is probably en route with a large force as we speak."

He didn't sound very convinced, but his kiss helped to calm my nerves so that I could think rationally. Realistically, I knew there was no way we could escape without being detected. I took a deep breath and settled back into the warmth of Danny's arms and drifted off to sleep.

10

I dreamed that night of home. I was back at our house on the
Nolichucky and everyone was there: Ma and Pa, Elizabeth, Luke,
Ben and Becky, Grandma and Grandpa. It was Christmas and
we were just about to sit down to eat when Danny rode up to the
door calling my name, "Samantha. Hey, Samantha." I suddenly
and reluctantly awoke from my dream when I realized Danny
was really calling my name.

"Samantha, look!" I heard hammering and looked over the
wall to see what he was watching so intently. The Mexicans were
building something. I couldn't tell what it was at first, but then
two of them picked up one of the objects and carried it over to
stack it with several others…siege ladders. They were building
siege ladders for scaling walls. Danny and I looked at each other
apprehensively. We had just been afforded a glimpse of Santa
Anna's plans. The final major attack on the Alamo would happen
soon. We ran to Colonel Travis's quarters to report what we
had seen. He brought his spy glass to assess the situation for
himself. The grim look on his face told us he had come to the
same conclusion.

Everyone in the Alamo ate their breakfast in silence that
morning, their eyes intently fixed on the main gate. I hoped and
prayed all day for reinforcements, but no one came. Finally that
afternoon, Colonel Travis ordered all the men to report to the

parade ground. Four men brought Colonel Bowie out on his cot so he could hear what Colonel Travis had to say. I stood at the back of the formation trying to remain as inconspicuous as possible, hoping against hope that the Colonel had received some late report stating that reinforcements were on the way. But my heart sank when I saw the look on Colonel Travis's face.

I felt sorry for Colonel Travis. He looked so young, so vulnerable standing there waiting for everyone to assemble. He had been so sure, so confident with that confidence that comes from being young and inexperienced that reinforcements would flock to the aid of so just a cause as defending the Alamo, the very gateway into Texas. He could not understand the cooler calculations of older men like Houston who could see the much larger picture; a picture depicting the need for time, the time to establish a government and raise and train an army that would at least stand a chance against Santa Anna's well trained masses. For those in the Alamo, the title of this picture was sacrifice and death.

Colonel Travis paced in front of our group for a few minutes collecting his thoughts. Finally, he said, "I know this has probably been the most trying twelve days most of you and your families have ever experienced, and I am very proud of the way you all have behaved and performed your duties under these conditions. I wish I could say that I have good news and reinforcements are on the way. I have sent several dispatches to Goliad, the Texian government which is now at Washington-on-the-Brazos, and the United States, but to no avail.

"I greatly regret that I must tell you I believe no help is coming. The enemy, on the other hand, has been receiving reinforcements daily and now numbers in the thousands. Our situation is dire; most probably hopeless."

Here he stopped to clear his throat, and to my surprise, I could see tears in his eyes. He paused for a moment, and then continued. "Texas has been a chance for me to obtain land and success, and to lead a better life. I think she has been the same for many of you. For me personally, I am prepared to stay here in the Alamo and defend her until my final breath. But if any of you would like to try to leave, you may do so. Santa Anna has dictated that surrender is not an option, but it may be possible to escape through the enemies' lines under cover of darkness." He stopped, pulled out his sword, and drew a line in the sand. "But if any of you are willing to stay with me here in the Alamo and fight to defend the cause of liberty and freedom for Texas, cross this line. I promise you we will sell our lives as dearly as possible."

One by one, all of the men, including Colonel Bowie who had the four men carry his cot, crossed over Travis's line except Moses Rose. Colonel Bowie was then taken to the baptistry in the chapel. That night Mr. Rose jumped over the north wall and disappeared into the darkness. I never heard whether he made it or not.

That afternoon, Colonel Travis summoned me to his quarters. When I entered, he was in the process of writing a letter.

"Please give me one moment, Mrs. Autry, to finish this letter to my son." Finally, he looked up. "Mrs. Autry, I have one last request to make of you."

"Yes, sir?" I asked. "And please call me Samantha, sir."

"Would you please go find Mrs. Dickinson and ask her to bring her daughter to my office? I want little Emily to have this." He held up a piece of string supporting the hammered gold ring with the tiger eye stone that I had always seen him wear.

He must have noticed my puzzled expression because he explained, "Little Emily reminds me of my own daughter back in Alabama."

"I knew you had a son here in Texas, but I didn't know you had a daughter, sir," I replied. I wanted to suggest he save it for his own daughter whom he might see someday, but we both knew this would never happen. Instead I asked, "Do you miss your children, sir?"

He gave me a sharp look as if I had overstepped my bounds in asking this question, but then his gaze softened and he sighed.

"I do miss them, Samantha, and I regret my divorce and all the unhappy circumstances that led to it. I thought I would have a chance to make up for some of the pain my absence has caused my children, but it seems that will not be the case." He looked extremely sad as he stared off into the distance.

"I'm so sorry," I said as I got up to leave. On an impulse, I walked to his side and laid a sympathetic hand on his shoulder. He covered it momentarily with his own, then withdrew it as I turned to walk out of the door.

I found Mrs. Dickinson with her husband in an intense conversation outside of the chapel while little Emily played at their feet. I noticed Mrs. Dickinson had tears in her eyes and I hesitated to approach them. Finally, I cleared my throat loudly as I walked up to them to signal my approach.

"Good afternoon," I said awkwardly. "Mrs. Dickinson, Colonel Travis sent me to find you and ask you to bring Emily to his office. He has something very special that he would like to give to her." Tears clouded my vision and I could no longer speak because of the lump in my throat. I just gave Mrs. Dickinson a hug, patted Mr. Dickinson's arm, and kissed little Emily on the top of her head. The smell of her hair reminded me so much of Becky that I had to hurry away before I completely lost control of my emotions.

Things remained relatively quiet for the rest of that day and all of the next. The Mexicans ceased their incessant shelling. I assumed they were saving their energy and resources for their major assault. The men in the Alamo spent their time writing their last letters to their families, making ammunition, and getting ready for the huge assault we all knew was coming. Mrs. Dickinson had agreed to take the letters with her if she and Emily were not taken prisoner and allowed to return to Gonzales. I had brought the last of the paper I had bought in Memphis, and

Danny and I both wrote letters home. That night before we went to sleep, he also gave me my lecture on staying out of the fighting.

"Samantha, when the battle starts, I want you to go shelter in the chapel with the women." I just looked at him as if he had lost his mind and he began to get angry. "Samantha, I mean it, damn it, I mean it!" Tears began to fill his eyes and mine too.

"Danny, you know I can't leave you. I just can't. Wherever you go, I go. Whatever happens to you, happens to me. That's just the way I am. You knew that when you married me. It's pointless to try to change me now."

He put his arms around me and hugged me closely realizing it was useless to try to change my mind and not wanting to fight on what could be our last night together. Then he gave me a long kiss. "I have something for you," he said softly. "I was saving it for our first anniversary, but I'm thinking I'd better give it to you now."

He reached into his pocket and pulled out the most beautiful gold locket I had ever seen. It was a pure gold locket hanging on a gold chain. The front of the locket was inscribed with Danny and Sam, and on the back was inscribed "forever." That was it—I started crying and couldn't stop.

"It's beautiful!" I sobbed. "When—"

"I ordered it before I came to Bexar last winter and picked it up when I got back. Zumwalt did a great job with the engraving, didn't he?"

"Yes, he did," I managed to say. I smiled up at Danny as he put the locket around my neck.

"I love you so much, Samantha Russell Autry," Danny whispered in my ear as he hooked the clasp.

"I love you so much also, Daniel Lee Autry," I said as I turned to face him. Since everyone figured the Mexican attack was eminent, Danny had been assigned to help guard the palisade with Colonel Crockett's men. Danny sat down and leaned back into a corner formed by the palisade and the chapel wall, and I settled back into his strong arms pulling our blanket up around us. For once, the night was peaceful and we slipped into a deep restful sleep. It would be the last restful sleep I would have for a very long time...and the last I would ever share with Danny.

11

Sometime during the early morning darkness, I sat bolt upright. Something, I wasn't sure what, had awakened me. I looked at Danny who was still asleep, then quickly surveyed the rest of the grounds. No movement; nothing. I had just settled back down when I heard it quite clearly this time; the snapping of twigs just outside the palisade wall. My heart began to thump as I got up and moved quietly to the wall. Peering through the lookout hole in the wall, my heart froze. I could see hundreds of Mexican soldados moving toward our position through the darkness.

For what seemed an eternity, I couldn't force myself to move or speak. I stood frozen with fear. Finally, I managed to yell, "Wake up, wake up, the Mexicans are attacking!" Danny, Colonel Crockett, and the other Tennesseans jumped up, grabbed their rifles, and began shooting over the palisade wall. The Mexicans, realizing they had lost the element of surprise, began yelling, "Vive Santa Anna, Vive Mexico," and began their charge in earnest, running at full speed toward our position. Their deafening cries were accompanied by the chilling melody of the "Deguello."

"Damn it, Samantha, get in the chapel, now!" I heard Danny yell over the din of rifle fire. I just ignored him, handed him his other rifle, grabbed the one he had just shot, and reloaded it. Pretty soon, it became a sort of morbid routine—shoot, hand off the loaded rifle, reload the spent rifle, shoot again. I managed to keep somewhat calm despite the earsplitting noise of cannons blasting, rifles cracking, and the acrid smelling smoke that threatened to choke me with every breath. But soon I began to hear the moans and screams of men being shot and my hands started to shake.

Danny had long since given up on trying to get me to go shelter with the women, and was doing his best to keep my mind on the task at hand—keeping us alive. "Come on, Samantha, focus. Load the rifle."

But I was finding it increasingly hard to focus. I saw Colonel Travis running to the north wall yelling, "Come on men, the Mexicans are upon us." I saw him climb the ramp to help fire the eighteen-pounder on the northwest corner with Joe by his side. "Samantha!" Danny yelled. I returned my attention to loading rifles. When I looked up again, I wished I hadn't. As I glanced in their direction, I watched in slow motion as Colonel Travis fell backward from what looked at this angle like a bullet right in his forehead. I felt tears begin to well up in my eyes, but I quickly wiped them away and got back to work.

It seemed every nerve in my body began a fearful vibration in unison to the constant pounding and firing of the cannons and rifles. I was glad I hadn't eaten anything, because I felt nauseated with fear. The screams of men dying on the other side of the palisade wall were becoming harder to stand. I was almost on the verge of running somewhere, anywhere away from this nightmare when the frequency of cannon and rifle fire began to slow and finally cease. I peered through the lookout hole and through the darkness and smoky haze, saw the Mexicans retreating from the walls. We had stopped them! Relief flooded through me as I turned to hug Danny. Maybe the Mexicans would give up and go away.

Just then, young Enrique Esparza ran out of the chapel screaming and crying, " I want my Papa! I want to fight!" His mother was behind him screaming for him to come back inside. I quickly jumped up, ran toward him, and caught him in midstride. Despite the panic threatening to choke my voice, I managed to calmly say, "You have to go back to your mother and protect her. It's what your father wants you to do." With tears streaming down his face, he reluctantly ran back to his mother. I gave her a look that reflected the fear and sorrow I saw in her eyes, then quickly turned and ran back to Danny.

My relief at the Mexican retreat was short-lived. The Mexicans hadn't given up. They had just paused long enough to change direction and concentrate their attack on the north and western walls where we didn't have as many cannon placements. In order to shoot from these walls, our boys had to stand above the protection of the walls and soon many Texians began to fall, including all of Juan Seguin's friends.

Seeing Texians fall and sensing that the tide had turned in their favor, the Mexicans began a vigorously renewed attack on the palisade wall. Soon Tennesseans began to fall. I screamed as I watched William fall with a shot through the chest. As I jumped up to go see about him, I managed to catch Uncle Micajah as he fell from a shot in the stomach.

"Goodbye, my girl" he gasped as he died in my arms. That was all I could take. I began to cry hysterically, until Danny began shaking me by the shoulders, "Samantha, Samantha, pull it together, I need you!" That helped some. I managed to pull myself together and start reloading Danny's rifles.

Powder...ball in patch...ram it home...powder in firing pan. The monotony of the motions helped to calm my nerves some. But the ear shattering cannon pounding and rifle fire continued to grow in an urgent crescendo, and the light created by the cannon's fiery spheres of death turned the early morning darkness into day.

Just at that moment, I understood why the shooting was becoming more desperate. I saw the tops of siege ladders appear over the tops of the north and west walls as the Mexicans breached our defenses and began pouring over the walls and onto the parade ground. I watched in horror as hundreds of Mexican soldiers emerged through the darkness and the dense rifle smoke, shooting and bayonetting any Texian in their path. They were closely followed by large, ominous looking Mexican soldados carrying axes and hacking down walls, doors, barricades, Texians, anything and anyone who stood in their way. From the corner of my eye, I saw some of these soldados enter the chapel where Colonel Bowie had been placed for what little protection might be available to him in his weakened condition. I felt sick but was momentarily filled with satisfaction when I heard multiple shots coming from that direction. I knew Colonel Bowie had taken out some of the enemy before they killed him.

My concern for Colonel Bowie was suddenly replaced by paralyzing horror. I saw several soldados advancing toward us. The flash of simultaneously fired rifles seemed to unite three more of Colonel Crockett's men and three Mexican soldados in a macabre dance of death before they all crumpled to the ground. Colonel Crockett and two men whom I didn't recognize were the only Tennesseans left. Just then six more soldados rushed out of the smoke filled darkness. Colonel Crockett and his men had no time to reload, and I watched in horror as the soldados first shot and then began to club them with their rifles. Even though he was shot, Colonel Crockett gave me one last sad, desperate look. Then letting out a mighty yell, he clubbed five soldados to death before being clubbed to death himself. Shocked at what had just happened, my eyes slowly traveled from the fallen Tennesseans to look up at that lone Mexican soldado looming out of the darkness to my left with murder in his eyes. He stopped right in front of Danny and me with his rifle aimed straight at Danny. The rifle exploded and Danny fell back into my arms. I just stared at him unable to comprehend what had just happened. My Danny was dead. My mind exploded with rage as I raised the rifle I had just reloaded and aimed it at the soldado. Before I could fire, something hit me in the back of the head and everything went dark.

When I finally came to, the sun was up. Its bright light blinded me as I tried to focus on what was going on around me.

My head hurt so badly, I could hardly sit up, let alone think, so I concentrated on the first task. I finally managed to sit up and look around. My heart sank as I surveyed the scene around me. The Mexican soldados were dragging the bodies of Texians outside the gate and stacking them in piles. I could just see two piles through the main gate. I realized with horror that they planned to burn the bodies so that they would not have a proper burial. I looked around for Danny's body but it was gone, buried under other bodies in one of the piles.

With tears coursing down my face, I managed to stand shakily. At that moment rough hands grabbed me and dragged me outside the gate. My hands were quickly tied behind my back, and I was shoved to my knees at the feet of El Presidente himself surrounded by several of his officers. I noticed the other women from the Alamo were being provided mules for transportation. I assumed Santa Anna was sending them to Gonzales. I saw Joe leading Mrs. Dickinson's mule with poor little Emily screaming and crying. Sam, Betty, and the other women and children followed behind. I was glad that they were going to be allowed to leave even though I figured there was a good chance I would not be afforded the same opportunity. I really didn't care. I felt dead inside. So dead that I was sure I would never ever be able to experience any more emotion as long as I lived. At that moment I could have cared less whether I lived or died.

Santa Anna spoke something to me in Spanish which I did not understand. One of his officers interpreted it for me. "His Excellency wants to know why you were fighting and not in the chapel with the women."

I looked Santa Ann squarely in the eyes. "Tell his Excellency that I was not about to leave my husband's side when I could be of assistance to him in the fighting. That makes me an enemy combatant, so I suppose, under the terms you dictated, you will have to kill me."

Santa Anna looked surprised. I guess he expected me to be begging for my life. He said something else which the officer translated, "You do not seem to care whether you live or die."

I answered, "You're right. I don't care. In fact, I believe I would rather die. But before I do, I have one question for your men. Why do you fight for a disgusting, murderous, cruel tyrant whose only desire is to oppress your people and make your lives miserable?" The officer looked at me in surprise and hesitated. "Go ahead," I demanded. "Ask the question. I really want to know so that maybe I can understand the purpose for all of this senseless killing."

The officer turned and directed my question to the other officers and to El Presidente. I never got an answer, but I noticed the officers either looked at the ground or looked away from me to avoid answering. It didn't matter. I knew I had forced them to face an unpleasant truth. Also, I had definitely struck a nerve with El Diablo Presidente. He flew into a rage and ordered his men to kill me. I could tell because three of them drew their swords. One officer, an older gentlemen, pleaded for Santa Anna to spare my life. I guessed that, as a rule, most Mexican officers weren't very keen on executing a woman. Santa Anna relented and withdrew his order.

Just at that moment, a small spark began to burn in the pit of my stomach as pictures of Colonel Crockett, Colonel Travis, Uncle Micajah, Juan's friends, my Danny dying, and young Enrique screaming and crying for his father flashed before my eyes. The spark soon grew into a fiery rage.

"Please tell El Presidente one more thing for me," I snarled.

"And what would that be?" the officer asked condescendingly.

I looked Santa Anna directly in the eye and said, "You will regret letting me live."

12

"Wake up, my little sleepy head," Danny whispered in my ear as he softly kissed my cheek. I smiled sleepily and opened my eyes. I immediately wished I hadn't. The harsh glaring sun and cold wind jolted me back to the hard reality that Danny was dead and I had been dreaming.

I sat up gingerly, rubbing the back of my aching head. Although my body seemed unable to shake off the cold numbness that permeated it, my heart sprang to life with a stabbing pain that filled my eyes with tears. I leaned against one of the trees in the copse into which I had stumbled after my confrontation with El Diablo Presidente. There I sobbed for what seemed like hours, and through those hot, painful tears watched the smoke rise from the burning pyres of Texian dead and slowly drift southward in the stiff northerly wind.

I cried until I had no tears left and only racking sobs continued to escape my throat. Finally I could cry no more, and that merciful numbness that enveloped my body seeped into my heart. I stood up slowly and began walking along the road out of San Antonio de Bexar toward Gonzales.

About a mile down the road, I came upon an abandoned jacal. It looked as if the Mexican family living there had hurriedly left that morning probably when they realized the Alamo was about to fall and Santa Anna would soon invade all of the surrounding territory. Inside the small hut, I found a dish of tortillas still on the kitchen table. My stomach began to rumble, so I grabbed several of the tortillas and began stuffing them into my mouth. There was nothing else of value to me left in the house except a sombrero and an old water skin but out back, I found a pair of pants, and a shirt hanging from a piece of rope stretched between two trees. Amazingly enough, they were just about my size! I guess they belonged to a boy in the family.

I found a bucket by the family's well and filled it with water from which I gulped thirstily, then proceeded to wash my face, hands and arms. I soon realized that my clothes were spattered with blood, Danny's blood, and my eyes began to cloud with tears. I wiped my eyes, took off my soiled clothes, washed off as best I could, and put on the pants and shirt. Then I tore a small piece of cloth from the bottom of the shirt and wrapped it around the remaining tortillas, filled the water skin with water, crammed the sombrero on my head, and headed down the road toward Gonzales. My heart filled with hot rage at the Mexican Santanistas, even as my head began to coolly form a plan. As I walked, that hot rage finally burned itself out leaving my heart burnished in cold revenge.

I alternately ran and walked, only stopping to sleep for a few hours during the night. I knew I had to hurry because I was already almost two days behind Mrs. Dickinson's party, and I hoped to reach Gonzales on the same day as they did. I figured General Houston might be there, trying to raise an army in the hopes of relieving the Alamo. Of course, he would be informed that it was too late to save the Alamo, and I wanted to be there when the general decided on his next move.

Instead of going straight into town, I stopped by our house. It had not been disturbed in our absence, being so far out of town, and the sight of it tore at my heart. Danny and I would never get to enjoy our home together. I almost broke down again at the thought of Danny, but quickly focused my mind on the next steps of my plan. I dug out my sewing kit and took out the scissors. I went outside and, hesitating only momentarily, began cutting off all my hair until its length touched the bottom of my neck. It had to be short because I didn't know when I would get the chance to cut it again. I then went into the bedroom and found a pair of Danny's pants and a shirt, cut off the hems of the pant legs and cuffs of the shirt sleeves to fit my size, and quickly hemmed them back up. Then I found a pair of Danny's old boots and socks. Believe it or not, Danny and I almost wore the same size shoes. Ma always said I had big feet and Danny's feet were kind of small. We always made fun of each other because of this, and the thought brought tears to my eyes. God, I had to stop this! I angrily brushed back the tears and put on the altered clothes, socks, and boots.

I happened to glance by the door and see Danny's old floppy work hat hanging on a nail along with one of his old bags with a shoulder strap. I grabbed both of these and then went down to the cellar. I packed some jerky, apples, and dried peaches. I shoved the food, the Mexican clothes and sombrero, a blanket, and my slingshot into the bag. Danny had also left one rifle stored under our bed. He had told me about it before we left for San Antonio in January just in case I ever needed it when he wasn't around. I placed it and all the things I had packed beside our bed, then collapsed onto the bed and fell immediately into a deep, exhausted sleep.

I got up early the next morning, filled my water skin with water from our well and headed into Gonzales. My luck seemed to be holding because I arrived just in time to see General Houston escort Mrs. Dickinson into the general store. When the people of Gonzales heard what had happened to the Alamo, pandemonium ensued. Many of these people, my friends, had lost love ones at the Alamo, and their screams of anguish filled the air. I longed to comfort them, but I needed to remain unnoticed in the background. I had to first learn what the general planned to do, and then figure out how to best carry out my plan.

I did not have to wait long. Less than an hour later, General Houston emerged from the store, his expression grim; his eyes hard with anger. This was my first chance to really study General Houston. He was over six feet tall with handsome features and light blue eyes. But right now with that grim expression and those flashing eyes, he seemed pretty scary. So I did my best to avoid his attention. Mrs. Dickinson had not only reported the events of the Alamo but had delivered a personal message from Santa Anna. The Mexican Army planned to march through Texas and destroy every town. Santa Anna was on his way. The general ordered his men to begin assisting the civilians of Gonzales in packing their belongings to leave town. Chaos reigned as distraught, frightened citizens rushed to pack their wagons and get out of Gonzales.

Early on the morning of March 14, General Houston with his small army of around 374 men and the citizens of Gonzales began their trek toward the Colorado River. As I followed along at the end of the line of Gonzales refugees, I witnessed a sight that further broke my heart and remained seared in my mind for the rest of my life. As the last of the wagons reached the edge of town, General Houston's scouts returned to burn it down. As memories of my wedding, friends, picnics, and parties flashed through my mind, the fires from Gonzales's burning buildings licked the predawn darkness with searing flames and a defiant, roaring fury. Santa Anna would find only ashes.

No one spoke much as we trudged through the morning hours toward the Colorado, but a sense of urgency permeated our procession. I knew everyone was wondering how far behind Santa Anna's army actually was and whether General Houston planned to engage him in battle. I also figured the general was hoping that Fannin was on his way from Goliad with his four hundred men.

During the next few days, I did my best to stay in the background. Most everyone thought I was just a young volunteer soldier. At night I figured it was safe to spread my blanket near one of the fires since no one could get a good look at my face in the dark. The men hunted game and the women worked as a team cooking for their families and Houston's small army, so I did not have to eat any of my meager rations during those first few days. I even managed to sneak a few extra pieces of bread or biscuits to add to my collection since I had eaten all of the tortillas I had confiscated from the abandoned jacal before leaving Gonzales. I kind of felt bad about this, but rationalized my petty theft by planning for my upcoming mission. You see, I had decided to spy on the Mexican Army for General Houston.

We finally reached Burnham's ferry on the Colorado River on March 17. The men were itching for a fight. I heard several of the men griping at the general. "General, we have to stop Santa Anna here. Your scout, Deaf Smith, says he is only fifteen miles away and is separated from Urrea and Sesma. Let's git him now!"

But the general refused. He burned Burnham's Ferry to slow down the Mexican Army, and we proceeded down the east bank of the river to Beason's Crossing. Here our luck began to change. We started getting more recruits and the army grew to about 1,400 men. Unfortunately, the weather decided not to cooperate. It began raining and continued to rain heavily for days. The Colorado River swelled way up over its banks, turning our trails and roads into quagmires. Although the rains made conditions miserable, they did prove providential. They slowed down the Mexican Army and allowed the general time to give us volunteers some much needed military training. Even though I was small, there were several other young boys that had signed up, so I managed to blend in. I kind of enjoyed all of the marching, and I especially enjoyed shooting Danny's rifle though we didn't shoot much since we were trying to conserve our ammunition.

Though the general's army consisted of mostly undisciplined volunteer soldiers, his scout troop was probably the best in the country. Erastus "Deaf" Smith and his son-in-law, Hendrick Arnold, belonged to a small, highly skilled contingent of scouts attached to Captain Henry Karnes' cavalry unit. I knew they had been riding out searching for Santa Anna's Army, because, after one such scouting foray, Captain Karnes rode into camp with a Mexican prisoner who let us know just how divided Santa Anna's Army really was. He had sent troops under General Gaona up the Old San Antonio Road to Nacogdoches and ordered General Ramirez y Sesma to head for Beason's Crossing with around seven hundred men. The men were excited! Finally, maybe the general would let them fight when Sesma arrived!

General Sesma and his miscreant army arrived at Beason's Crossing on March 21. We didn't worry very much about this since the Colorado was so swollen there was no way they could cross. The general did order his men to help the civilians pack up and move a mile or so away out of range of any potential fighting. Since it looked as if both sides were going to be stalemated for a while, I decided this might be a good time to see if I was really cut out to be a spy.

The next day after morning drills while the men paused for dinner, I slipped away and raced down to the river. I could feel my frustration level rise as I studied it. The river was indeed running well over its banks, and when I say running, I mean running! Waves of water carried tree limbs and other debris downstream at an alarming rate. How in the world was I going to get across that river?! Sound carries really well across water, so even over the roar of the racing river I could faintly hear military orders spoken in Spanish and the pounding and clanking of camp equipment and artillery being set up. My frustration level crescendoed to the point of anger. I *had* to get across that river and I *had* to do it tonight! I *had* to know what those Mexicans were up to!

I crept as quietly as possible down the riverbank doing my best to stay behind the trees and bushes lining its edges. My spirits continued to sink as I beheld nothing but racing water sweeping around bends in the river's bank, then plummeting over rocks midstream carrying its never ending burden of limbs and debris. About a half mile down, I stopped and stared not believing my eyes. I had stumbled upon a spot where the river bank jutted out into the river about ten feet significantly narrowing the gap between it and the opposite bank. A tree had toppled over from the other side into the river further narrowing the distance between the two banks. Piles of debris had been caught by the branches of the tree forming a kind of bridge across the fallen tree. The distance from the bank to the tree looked to be only about six feet. All I had to do was to get across that small distance, and I could climb across the fallen tree to the shore. Danny and I had spent all our summers growing up swimming the Nolichucky and I was a good swimmer. I knew I could do this!

That evening I quickly changed into the Mexican clothes I had taken when I left Bexar. I then packed some jerky, two apples, the sombrero and my slingshot into a smaller bag I had found abandoned around camp, stored the rest of my belongings in the back of one of the supply wagons, and headed for the river. I soon found my crossing spot and jumped into the river. The current was strong, but I managed to make progress toward the fallen tree. I was about halfway across when suddenly the current strengthened and frigid waves began washing over my head. I felt myself being tugged off course and down under the water! I could hear the water roar in my ears, and feel the violent tug of the current like a heavy weight pulling me toward the bottom!

I willed myself not to panic as the fishy, silt laden water flooded my mouth. I kicked hard and managed to get my head above the water long enough to catch my breath and get my bearings. Luckily the current hadn't pulled me too far off course, and I had only drifted about ten yards from the tree. I swam as hard as I could and finally managed to get out of the middle of the river and away from the current. With the last of my energy, I managed to swim to the safety of the tree's waterlogged, though still sturdy, branches.

As I clung to the tree catching my breath, I could hear Sesma's army preparing for the evening and smell the beckoning odor of beans and tortillas along with roasting meat. I scrambled through the branches of the tree onto its trunk and crawled along the trunk toward the bank. When I reached the bank, I paused behind some bushes for a few minutes to catch my breath and regain my bearings. Then I began to slip through the woods as quietly as possible toward the sounds of the Mexican camp.

Darkness had fallen and the fires from the Mexican camp formed huge ghostly shadows against the trees. But the sight that caught my attention was the size of the camp! Sesma must have had about eight hundred or nine hundred soldados along with all of the camp followers, women who followed along with the Mexican army and cooked for them. I found some bushes near the edge of camp and soon spotted the tents where I figured Sesma and his officers were planning their next moves. I had to get near those tents! I crammed the still damp sombrero down low on my head, took a deep breath, and strolled through the camp as if I belonged there. Surprisingly no one paid any attention to me as they were all so busy cooking, eating, and cleaning up supper dishes. I strolled nonchalantly toward the tents, and then quickly ducked into some bushes directly behind them.

Fortune seems to favor the inexperienced and foolish because I inadvertently found myself in the most perfect spot! Plenty of good bushes for hiding surrounded the tent, and there were no camp fires around to illuminate my position. Also Sesma and his officers proved to be very talkative probably due to the consumption of copious amounts of tequila. My only problem proved to be my limited knowledge of Spanish even though Mrs. Garcia had taught me many basic words and phrases. I knew I would have to listen very carefully to pick up as many words as I could understand and remember.

Unfortunately, I was not disappointed. The first words I heard were something like *"Fannin y sus hombres capturados por Urrea."* I figured that meant Fannin and his men had been captured and would probably be killed if El Diablo Presidente had anything to do with it. The general would not be happy about this. Then I heard, *"General Tolsa, estamos en la communicacion con Gaona y Urrea. Urea tiene mil quinientos hombres y Gaona setecientos sincuenta. Ellos no estan lejos."* This sounded like Sesma had communicated with Gaona and Urrea. The rest, I was pretty sure, meant that Urrea had fifteen hundred men and Gaona had 750 and were not far away. The reason there were so many soldados here was that General Tolsa had arrived with his army! He must have just gotten here a few days ago because I knew the general didn't know about his arrival! Good Lord! I had to get back and tell the general!

Actually, this was the part of my plan I hadn't quite figured out. I had to find someone in Deaf Smith's company that I could communicate with without giving away my identity and I had to make them believe what I said. Suddenly I had an inspiration, a dangerous inspiration—an inspiration that might yet succeed in turning me into one of El Diablo Presidente's victims.

I waited patiently behind the tent and tried to pick up more information. Sesma, Tolsa, and their officers talked for a while longer but I couldn't make out what they were saying. I guess the tequila and the lateness of the hour finally began to affect them, because I heard the tent flap open and men leaving. Cautiously, I lifted the bottom of the tent and peered inside. Several lanterns illuminated its interior. In the middle stood a makeshift table made of crates with four crates positioned around it serving as chairs. On the table was a large map of Tejas y Coahuila with several pieces of paper scattered over its surface. Fortune continued to favor me as I figured she would since, at that moment, I didn't think there existed another person in this world as foolish as me. I took a deep breath, quickly slipped under the bottom of the tent and grabbed one of the papers tucked underneath several of the others. Then I just as quickly slipped back out under the tent bottom and flew back to the safety of the bushes lining the riverbank.

I spent the rest of the night fitfully catnapping next to a tree down by the riverbank. I opened my eyes to an overcast gray dawn and the smell of frying tortillas from the Mexican camp. A quick glance at the sky let me know that the rain would soon return and with it a rough river crossing. I needed to get back across and back to our camp soon, but first I wanted to make a quick survey of the Mexican artillery. I crept as silently as possible to the edge of the Mexican camp and crouched behind some bushes. My stomach began to rumble, so I pulled some jerky out of my bag and absently munched on it as I studied the Mexican encampment in the daylight. Our forces were pretty evenly matched as far as actual troop numbers, but they did have one very significant advantage: two field cannon. The general would definitely need to know about this also since he was getting a lot of pressure from his men to attack Sesma.

As I ran back to my crossing spot, I tried to plan how I was going to get my information to General Houston without revealing my identity. I had my piece of evidence double wrapped in strips of cloth and stuck inside the sombrero in my bag. I prayed it would stay dry during my swim. But I couldn't figure out whom to give it to. Oh well, things had worked out so far. Hopefully, they would continue to do so.

The river had slowed considerably, so I managed to swim the six feet without incident and even managed to keep my bag mostly out of the water by keeping it somewhat balanced on top of my head. When I finally made it to our side of the river, I clambered on to the bank and fell to my knees. My legs felt like rubber and I felt myself gasping for air. It was then that I realized how nervous and scared I had actually been during my little spying escapade. After a few minutes, I felt some strength return to my legs and my breathing return to normal. I got to my feet and headed for camp.

As I approached camp, I could tell things were not going well for the general. I grabbed my belongings from the back of the supply wagon where I had hidden them and changed my clothes. This wagon was turning out to be a great hiding spot. I took out the Mexican paper but quickly stuffed everything else back into the wagon. Then I headed toward the general's tent still unsure of what I was going to do. I could hear men's angry voices complaining about the general's lack of action.

At that moment, both fortune and her counterpart decided to bless me with their presence at the same time. Since I am somewhat of a pessimist, I'll relate the bad part first. As I headed toward the general's tent, who should I see going in to meet with him? None other than Juan Seguin! Heck! I had forgotten that Travis had sent him to report the Alamo situation to the general. On second thought, it was a wonder that I hadn't run into him earlier. So now I had the added problem of trying to stay out of his sight. I knew if he saw me, he would surely recognize me and probably turn me in to the general.

I unconsciously began backing away from the general's tent and while doing so, backed right squarely into a large, tall figure. I slowly turned around, and looked up wide-eyed until I met the stern yet somewhat amused gaze of a boyishly nice-looking black man. I recognized him as Sergeant Hendrick Arnold, Deaf Smith's son-in-law and one of the general's expert scouts.

I quickly lowered my gaze and my voice, "Mornin', sir."

"Mornin," he returned congenially. Then, as I continued to stand right in front of him, he asked, "Anything I can do for you, son?"

I relaxed when I realized my disguise was working. "Actually, sir, there is." I decided to go for broke and tell him exactly what

I had done. "You see, sir, yesterday I crossed the river and went to spy on Sesma's Army and I have some news to report. The problem is I know the general is busy, and frankly, I'm not sure he would listen to somebody like me. So I was hoping I could tell you and you could report for me, since you are one of his best scouts." I hoped the flattery would help my cause.

He gave me a very skeptical yet indulgent grin. "You swam across that river and spied on Sesma yesterday without getting caught?"

"Yes, sir," I said, relieved. Maybe he would believe me. "I found a place where the bank sticks out about ten feet and there was a fallen tree on the other side that narrowed the gap, and I swam across. Then, when it got dark, I crept up behind Ol' General Sesma's tent and hid in some bushes so I could listen to what Sesma and his officers were saying."

He continued to grin at me indulgently. "And just how did you get through the camp to Sesma's tent."

This was where I had to admit about taking the Mexican's clothes in Bexar. I didn't want to tell him my entire story, so I just hung my head ashamedly and said, "I stole some Mexican clothes from an abandoned jacal on my way to Gonzales. Sesma's soldados didn't even take any notice of me," I finished proudly.

The skepticism began to leave his face and it was then that I decided to produce my evidence. I showed him the paper I had taken from Sesma's tent. I had never seen anyone's expression change so quickly. His turned to surprise in a flash as he read the paper. I hadn't studied the paper until now since it was all in Spanish and I had had very little practice in reading Spanish, but now I noticed it had El Diablo Presidente's signature on it! I decided right then that fortune must indeed consider me the most foolish person in the world!

I figured out Hendrick must be quite fluent in Spanish because he quickly read the letter and then began to ask me questions. I told him what I had heard Sesma say about Fannin, Gaona, and

Urrea in Spanish as well as I could remember and what I figured it meant. I told him about Tolsa's reinforcements arriving and about the two cannon. Hendrick gave me an admiring look and squeezed my shoulder, then hurried off to the general's tent. I waited a few minutes and was about to go get some breakfast when Hendrick and the general emerged from the tent. Hendrick looked in my direction as he continued talking to the general. Then, of course, the general looked in my direction also. I froze under his piercing gaze, and for just a second, I feared that gaze had penetrated my disguise. I quickly dropped my gaze and hurried off to the chow line.

13

My euphoria over the success of my spying expedition did not last long. After breakfast, the rains returned dampening everyone's spirits which resulted in an increase in the grumbling. The grumbling lessened considerably with the arrival of four supply wagons from some nearby black farmers. We finally had something to eat besides jerky and stale bread! I had noticed several free black men among our ranks besides Hendrick, and the supplies provided by black farmers during our retreat often saved the general from dealing with wholesale desertion. It lifted my spirits to see the different cultures—black, Tejano, and white—all fighting for the same goal: freedom from an oppressor. It was so different from what I had seen in the United States.

Hendrick told me during breakfast that the paper I stolen from Sesma had indeed turned out to be a letter from Santa Anna informing Sesma that he was on his way with some troops from San Antonio and would be joining Sesma at the Colorado River by the beginning of April. In the letter Santa Anna also gloated about the fact that he had ordered Urrea to execute Fannin and his men. God I hated that man! Because of my report, the general decided to break camp and continue our retreat toward San Felipe de Austin. Needless to say, the men were not happy. They wanted to fight badly. They began calling the general a coward and several more men deserted.

After supper that evening, Hendrick came to tell me that the general wanted to see me. My heart plummeted to the pit of my stomach and then shot back up so far into my throat that I thought I was going to choke. I did my best not to let Hendrick see my panic as I headed toward the general's tent. Before announcing my presence I made sure that Danny's buckskin shirt hung loosely in front and that my hat was firmly crammed down on my head. Hopefully, the general would meet me outside the tent and I wouldn't have to remove my hat.

The general stepped outside the tent just as I walked up.

"Private Autry reporting as directed, sir," I announced in my lowered voice as I sharply saluted.

"Private Autry," the general said as he returned my salute, "I understand you went on a little spy mission without orders or permission." His stern expression and hard blue eyes intimidated me, and I subconsciously dropped my gaze.

"Yes, sir, I did," I replied. "I meant no disrespect, sir. I was only trying to help our cause by gaining some additional intelligence."

His stern expression never changed, but I thought I saw his mouth slightly twitch with a brief ghost of a smile. "Your information proved very informative, so no punishment will be administered at this time. But if you continue to take it upon yourself to do *anything* beyond what you are ordered, I will be forced to administer punishment. Do you understand, Private?"

"Yes, sir!"

"You are dismissed."

I saluted, somehow managed to do an about face on my rubbery legs, and headed back to my campfire. Only when I had unceremoniously plopped down near its warmth did I allow myself to breathe again. Despite the small, niggling doubt gnawing at the pit of my stomach after being subjected to that penetrating, inscrutable gaze, I felt pretty sure the General hadn't seen through my disguise. Hopefully, my luck would last.

The next morning we began our retreat to Felipe de Austin in the middle of a torrential downpour. Actually I was glad it was raining because it helped to hide the tears streaming down my face. I kept my hat pulled down low so no one would notice. For some reason today, I felt very sad and depressed. I knew the incessant rain and men grumbling were probably contributing to my mood, but they weren't the real reason for my depression. The fact was my heart still ached badly for my Danny and probably would for a very long time.

Just at that moment, Hendrick rode up beside me on his big quarter horse. He seemed pretty excited, so to take my mind off of Danny, I asked him what was going on.

"Sam, the general ordered me and Deaf to go back to the Colorado to wait around for Santy Anny. He wants to know how many days behind us that ol' devil is."

"Well, you—" I started to say "be careful," but thought that might sound like something a woman would say and so finished with, "Well, good luck." As he started to turn his horse around, a thought occurred to me. "Hendrick, how long have you been a part of this revolution?"

"Well, Sam, I guess I've been fightin in this here little war with Santy Anny almost since the beginnin'. I fought at Concepcion and then at Bexar with Ol' Ben Milam. Me and my buddy, Greenbury Logan both fought with Ol'Ben. I been wonderin' about Greenbury. He's like me, a free black man who came to Texas for the land and got a big ol' land grant in Stephen Austin's third colony, I believe. I wonder where that ol son-of-a-gun is?" he added thoughtfully.

My excitement grew as I listened to his reminiscences. "You didn't happen to know anyone in Captain Neill's artillery unit at Bexar, did you? My...friend, Daniel Autry, was in that unit!"

"I can't say that I did. If I remember rightly, Captain Neill's unit was outside the walls keepin' reinforcements from gettin' to the Mexicans. I was inside the town."

"I see," I said, a little disappointed. I guess I just wanted someone to talk with about Danny. "Well, I hope you find your friend pretty soon."

"And I hope you find your friend, Danny. Stay safe, Sam, see you in a few days." With that, he galloped off to join Deaf and the other scouts. As I watched him go, my streaming tears turned into a flood. Hopefully one day Hendrick would find his friend. I, on the other hand, would never see Danny again.

We reached San Felipe on the evening of March 28. The men just knew the general would wait for the Mexican Army to catch up to us there and then we would have a good old fight and send the Mexican Army packing back to Mexico. But after spending just one night in San Felipe, the general ordered us to pack up and move out. The men were furious! How could General Houston abandon San Felipe de Austin, Austin's first settlement, Texas's very birthplace! Captain Moseley Baker and Captain Wiley Martin refused to retreat and demanded the general let them stay and guard the San Felipe and Fort Bend Crossings. The general decided he couldn't stop them and so, with only five hundred men, he headed to Jared Groces's Plantation on the Brazos River.

But Baker and Martin weren't the only ones who remained at San Felipe. After thinking things through and realizing that my bout of depression wasn't going away any time soon and might actually draw unwanted attention to myself, I decided I would stay and do a little spying on my old nemesis, El Diablo Presidente. Since we knew now that he had left San Antonio de Bexar, I figured he would start chasing the Texian Army after joining Sesma at the Colorado River, and I knew he wouldn't be able to resist coming through San Felipe and burning it to the ground after sacking it for supplies. What I hadn't counted on was the citizens burning down the town. As soon as the Texian Army left, they began setting fire to all of the buildings before leaving. I managed to gather some food and fill some water skins with fresh water before they totally burned the town to the ground. Then I spent the night in an old barn that had managed to escape the conflagration.

The sight of San Felipe burning to the ground depressed me even further. My thoughts drifted back to when Danny and I first got to Texas and passed through San Felipe on our way to Gonzales. I could still hear Stephen Austin's voice rallying the folks by telling them about the tyrant Santa Anna, and how awed Danny had been by just hearing his voice. I felt the tears begin to run down my face and sobs choke my throat; tears for all those poor people who had lost their homes during this whole ordeal and tears for Danny. I cried for most of the night, but by morning I was all cried out and the familiar hardness had once again settled around my heart. El Diablo Presidente would pay. I would personally see to that!

14

The general and the rest of the army left San Felipe for Groces' Plantation on March 29 after spending only one day there with the men grumbling and griping vociferously about how unthinkable it was to abandon San Felipe, the birthplace of Texas, to the Mexicans. I understood, and I vowed to make the general's decision pay off in the long run. I would stay behind and glean all the information I could from El Diablo Presidente.

The sight of San Felipe's charred remains proved to only add to my general depression. So after scavenging everything I could from the town itself, I headed west of town to find a good hiding place to wait for El Presidente to arrive. I couldn't believe my luck when I found an abandoned farm house not far from the edge of town that had not been burned to the ground. I discovered some jerky, cornmeal, and apples in the cellar, along with some powder and shot. I guess the family didn't have room to pack it all in their hurry to leave. For the rest of that day, I watched the road thinking the Mexicans would surely be arriving soon, but I saw no one, not even a dog on the road. Finally I gave up watching, went inside, fixed myself some corn cakes to go along with my jerky and apples, and fell asleep on the cornhusk mattress the family had left in the front bedroom of the house.

Later that night, I discovered I was not the only Texian who had remained behind. I had just dozed off when I was awakened by the snorting and neighing of horses and men's voices and the smell of meat cooking. I got up and crept quietly along the river bank toward the source of the sounds. Across the river, a company of Texians had set up camp and were eating supper. What in the world! Then I remembered. Moseley Baker and his men had decided to remain behind and see if they could catch Santa Anna. I know this doesn't sound nice, but Captain Baker never was the sharpest tool in the shed. He was also very hotheaded. I could hear him clear across the river, and I was sure any Mexicans in the vicinity could hear him also.

"I'll be damned if I'm going to tuck tail and run from ol' Santy Anny like our yeller general." This brilliant remark was followed by a chorus of "Yea" and "We ain't runnin from no Mexicans."

Obviously, stupid captains ended up in command of stupid soldiers. Now it was imperative that I find out Santa Anna's location and warn Baker. I felt it was my obligation to the general to try to save Baker and his company from certain slaughter. The Texian Army needed every man it could get no matter how unintelligent, and I would not let Moseley squander his men on a futile attack. Maybe if I could confirm that Santa Anna had formed a pretty large force by joining up with Sesma and Tolsa, Baker would get some sense scared into him and retreat back to Groce's Plantation. I scurried back to my little house and tried to get a little more sleep before daylight.

I awoke before dawn the next morning in a near panic, sure that the Mexicans must be right outside my door, or at the very least, marching down the road in vast numbers. But as I gazed down the road expectantly, not a soul did I see. I kept looking out the window all that morning in surprised bewilderment. Where were the Mexicans? Surely they were right behind the general, ready to annihilate our army at the very first opportunity. I quickly packed my little bag with some food and two blankets I had found in the house and filled my water skin from the well. My thoughts were whirling so fast in my brain, they were tripping over themselves.

Where was the Mexican Army? What was going on? Was Santa Anna so arrogant and stupid that he thought he could just take his time? I donned my Mexican disguise and headed westward in search of El Diablo.

I moved at a slow run all that day and the next and finally caught up with the Mexicans that evening. A light rain had been falling for days turning the roads into a veritable quagmire and slowing the Mexican Army to a crawl. Santa Anna didn't seem to mind the slow pace though. He rode at the front of the column with an arrogantly serene expression on his face, seemingly oblivious to his men struggling to move their equipment and artillery through the mud. He must have been feeling pretty sure of his imminent success at squelching our little revolution. But why wasn't he in a hurry to catch up with the Texian Army and finish things off?

I shadowed their movements for the rest of that evening and the next day by keeping to the trees and brush along the side of the road, making mental notes about troop numbers and artillery power. That evening I hid in a dense thicket of yaupon bushes right outside of town so I could watch the Mexicans set up camp and see where Santa Anna would decide to have his sumptuously apportioned tent set up. I had never seen the likes of such a tent. It was huge! I watched as several soldados brought a table, chairs, and a bed for his Excellency. Several women rushed in and out bringing food and drinks for Santa Anna and his officers. I thought about the General's small mud-spattered tent and the bedroll that he unpacked every night from behind his saddle and spread out on the dirt. A spark of hatred flared inside my guts, but I quickly calmed myself down. I had to focus on what was being done in that tent, not the tent itself.

Santa Anna sent a scout into town to check things out. I knew, of course, El Diablo would be disappointed since there was nothing left of the town but charred remains. I was right. That night, after everyone in camp had settled down to sleep, I positioned myself in some brush at the back of Santa Anna's tent. I listened with hatred in my heart and hot tears flowing down my face as he described his victory at the Alamo. *"Probablemente perdio cerca de seis cientos de soldados. Los soldados son pollos. Se trataba de un pequeno asunto.*

That unfeeling, arrogant maniac didn't even care that he had lost six hundred of his best soldiers in the process of killing all my friends! They were nothing but chickens to him! God Almighty, he was going to pay, I swore softly to myself. He was going to pay big! I then heard something about Urrea and Matagorda Island. From the rest of the conversation, I figured that Urrea and his men were headed to Matagorda Island to block off any assistance the Texians might get from the coast.

Then I heard him say, *"En primer lugar, ir a San Felipe y luego a Fort Bend."* Fort Bend. So he definitely was headed to San Felipe and Baker. I had to get back to warn Baker. So that was why he was so unconcerned about their slow pace. Urrea was blocking any assistance that might come from the United States, and Santa Anna planned to take Fort Bend which would block off the Texian army from its government at Washington-on-the-Brazos. I had to try to talk Captain Baker into abandoning San Felipe and retreating to Groce's Plantation.

I wiped the tears from my face and slipped quietly under cover of darkness back to the road towards San Felipe. I did my best to stay within the woods along the road in the event Santa Anna decided to send out more scouts. The rain had stopped and a full moon was peaking from behind the clouds. Its silvery luminescence gave off just enough light for me to see where I was going.

I arrived back in San Felipe around midmorning of the next day, changed back into my buckskins, and headed straight for Baker's camp across the river. I found Baker sitting by a fire outside his tent melting lead for musket balls. I shoved my hat down low on my head and approached him my heart pounding loudly in my ears. I prayed he wouldn't see through my disguise.

After saluting briskly, I announced, "Private Autry reporting with intelligence concerning Mexican troop movements."

He looked at me with a rather dubious expression, and then told me to proceed with my report.

"Sir, Santa Anna is coming this direction with Sesma, Tolsa, and an army of at least 1,500 men. They will be here probably by late today. There is no way you will be able to stop them. They will slaughter you and your men."

"Private Autry, I don't know who you are or where you got your information, nor do I care. Nor do I care about the number of Mexicans Santa Anna is bringing with him. At the very best, we will lick them. At the very worst, we will put a hurt on them. Either way it goes, it don't matter because we are not runnin' from no Mexicans! Besides, General Sam ordered me to stay here and fight."

Frustration and rage were mounting inside me at his arrogance and stupidity. "Oh my God, have you lost your mind? The only reason he ordered you to stay here was because you kept giving him a hard time about retreating and demanded he give you permission to stay. I don't think you understand. Santa Anna is not coming here to throw you a party. He is a cruel, ruthless, sadistic tyrant. I know for a fact that he will slaughter every last one of you!" I paused to take a deep breath and try to calm myself down. "I think the prudent thing to do would be to retreat to Groces's Plantation and join the general."

I saw his eyes flash and his face flush with anger. "I will not retreat like our cowardly general. We will stay here and fight!"

I fought my anger and decided to try a different tact. "Sir, the general needs all the men he can get. I see no sense in getting all these men killed trying to save a town that has already been burned to the ground!" With that said, I turned on my heel and walked away without saluting. I could hear him calling me to come back and threatening to have me court martialed for disobedience and disrespect, but I just kept walking. People like him didn't deserve the time of day, much less respect, but I did feel sorry for his men.

I returned to my little house at San Felipe and waited for the Mexicans to arrive. I didn't think going back to the Mexican camp would prove any more profitable at this time, and so I decided to wait for them to come to me. I waited for two more days before the Mexican Army finally made it to San Felipe. Of course, they didn't stay because the town had been burned to the ground, so Santa Anna left Sesma with eight hundred men to deal with Baker. Although I felt a little better about Baker's chances now that Santa Anna had split up his forces, I didn't want to stay around to see the outcome of that totally unnecessary confrontation. I put on my Mexican clothes, packed some supplies and my blanket and set out to follow Santa Anna.

When Santa Anna's army reached Thompson's Ferry, they ran into a small problem. They needed the ferry to cross the Brazos River, but knew the ferry man would refuse to help them get across. Luckily for them and unlucky for the ferry man, one of Santa Anna's officers, Colonel Almonte, spoke perfect English and tricked the ferry man into bringing the ferry to their side of the river. The more I thought about it the more I felt pretty sure that Almonte had been my interpreter at the Alamo. After crossing the river, Santa Anna and his officers went into the town of Fort Bend. I saw Santa Anna speaking to several civilians with Almonte acting as interpreter but didn't dare get close enough to them to hear what they were saying. After a while, I headed back towards the Mexican camp outside of town.

I decided to stay around the fringes of the Mexican camp to wait for Santa Anna and his officers to return and possibly hear something useful. I didn't hear anything useful, but I did get the scare of my life. As I walked back toward the camp, I passed two Mexican soldados, both of whom had been at the Alamo. I quickly lowered my head and sped up my steps, but I could tell from the look on one of the soldado's faces that I looked familiar to him. He didn't turn around to look at me as I passed but went back to talking to his fellow soldado. I would have to be extra careful to stay away from them.

Santa Anna did return that evening and, of course, went straight to his luxurious tent. Soon his officers joined him, so I found some bushes near the tent, made myself comfortable and prepared to listen. I wasn't disappointed.

Santa Anna began, *"He escuchado algunos noticias interesantes hoy. El gobierno tejano ha dejado Washington-on-the-Brazos y se ha movido a Harrisburg. Mi plan es ir a Harrisburg y aniquilarlos."*

I couldn't believe it! It sounded as if he had said that the Texian government had moved to Harrisburg. And he planned to go there and…aniquilarlos. I wasn't sure what that meant, but I figured it wasn't good. That did it! I needed to get to Groces's Plantation and let the general know what was going on with Baker and the Texian government.

As I eased out of the bushes, I suddenly felt myself back into something solid. I turned around and saw the trousers and jacket of a Mexican uniform. My eyes traveled upward to the face of one of the soldados I had been trying to avoid. I watched the look in his eyes change from surprise to astonished anger as he recognized me. I tried to run, but he caught my shirt so suddenly that he threw me off balance and I fell to the ground. He began yelling "Traidor Tejano" and tried to pin my arms and legs to the ground with his hands and knees. Just before he managed to firmly pin down my left leg, I managed to pull it out from beneath him and kick him between the legs. As he rolled to the ground yelling and moaning, I jumped to my feet and took off at a dead run just as three of his fellow soldados came running to his aid.

I ran as hard and fast as I could down the road back to San Felipe. I could hear shouting back in the camp and paused for just a second to look back. The soldado had called for horses, and he and the three other soldados were waiting impatiently for them to be saddled. I knew I couldn't outrun those horses, so I dashed into the brush on the left side of the road and hid in the underbrush, praying they would ride by and not see me.

Just then I heard the frantic gallop of horses' hooves coming down the road, only they were coming from the opposite direction from the Mexican camp! My curiosity got the best of me, so I crept quietly up toward the edge of the brush to see who it was. Whoever it was, slowed down at about the spot where I had run into the woods. My heart pounding, I raised my head just enough to get a glimpse of the rider. Much to my surprise, it was Hendrick!

"Sergeant Arnold!" I called in a loud whisper. "It's me, Sam."

He looked a little surprised, then a grin spread across his face. "Sam! I'm mighty glad to see you! Jump up behind me! We've got to get outta here, before them Mexicans catch up to us."

I jumped up behind him and we took off at a dead gallop. Suddenly he veered off the road onto a small trail that I could barely see in the darkness. Obviously, Hendrick had been this way before. The Mexican soldados rode right past us! Hendrick finally let the horse slow to a walk when he felt sure we were far enough into the woods that we could not be seen.

"Hendrick, what are you doing here?" I asked.

"That was what I was going to ask you," he said, "but I'll go first. General Sam sent me to find out what had happened to Baker and his men. I caught up with them headed to Groces' Plantation. They had managed to get themselves into a little skirmish with ol Santy Anny right outside of San Felipe and got their backsides kicked. Good thing is, they only lost one man. Captain Baker had sense enough to retreat when he realized they couldn't hold the town. Ol' Wiley Martin and his men also came stragglin' in. I guess they ran into Santy Anny when he took Thompson's Ferry and crossed the river to get to Fort Bend. I decided to find out Santy Anny's exact position and was heading toward their camp when I saw you duck into those woods and those Mexicans chasing after you. Thank goodness there is a full moon and you had on that white Mexican peasant shirt or I might not have seen you at all. I'm glad you saw me when you did! That was a pretty close shave, boy! You almost got us both caught!"

"I'm real sorry, Hendrick. I've been spying on Santa Anna myself and have a lot to tell the general. Actually, I was going to tell it to you and have you tell him, since he'll skin me alive if he finds out I've been spying again. Oh, and thanks heaps for saving me from those Mexicans. I really don't know what I would have done if you hadn't come along."

I told Hendrick about hearing Santa Anna describe the massacre at the Alamo to Tolsa and Sesma. Somehow, I managed to do this without crying. I told him how they had entered San Felipe with about 1,500 men and when they found the town burned to the ground, they had decided to go to Fort Bend. I told him how they had captured Thompson's Ferry and crossed the river. I also told him about following Santa Anna and his officers into Fort Bend where Santa Anna found out that the Texian government had moved to Harrisburg. Lastly, I told him about Santa Anna's plans to take eight hundred men to Harrisburg to capture the Texian government, and how I almost got caught spying. "But please leave that last part out when you are reporting to the general if you can," I added. Then I asked how things were going at Groces' Plantation.

"Things are going pretty good there," said Hendrick. "We've finally had a chance to rest and train for battle. We've been gettin' plenty of supplies and food. The doctors have had time to treat the sick and get them well and, best of all, we've been getting reinforcements! I think the general mainly wanted us to rest up and train so Deaf and me haven't done any long-distance scouting missions. Our only missions have been to ride out a ways to see if Santy Anny was heading our way. All of us were puzzled about why he wasn't. But, thanks to you, we know why now." He had a look of grateful admiration in his eyes. "But don't you worry none, I won't tell the general where I got my information." We rode along in silence for a while and I noticed Hendrick had a kind of worried expression on his face.

"What's wrong, Hendrick?" I finally asked.

"Well, boy, actually the general has asked me where you were a couple of times since we got to Groces' Plantation."

I felt a chill surround my heart and spread throughout my body. I realized then that I was kind of afraid of the general. After all, he could be very intimidating. "I don't want to get you into trouble, Hendrick, so don't worry about covering for me. Just give him the information and, if he asks, tell him the truth. I'll try to stay out of his sight."

We reached San Felipe de Austin early the next morning and stopped at my little house long enough to give the horse a breather and allow me to change back into my buckskins. After eating a quick breakfast of cold biscuits and jerky provided by the always ever-prepared Hendrick, I packed the rest of my things, grabbed my rifle, and we headed out for Groces's Plantation.

We reached the Texian camp across from the plantation around noon, and found it in a state of organized chaos. The general had decided to move the army across the river using the Yellowstone, an old steamboat that had docked at Groce's landing. Because of all the chaos, nobody noticed me searching for the wagon where I had hidden all of my supplies. Luckily I found it before they loaded it onto the Yellowstone.

Everyone was running around loading equipment, supplies, and men, and best of all, two cannon the men had nicknamed the twin sisters that had been donated to us by some citizens from Cincinnati, Ohio. To my surprise, I saw Secretary of War Thomas Rusk dogging the general's every step. During the brief lunch break, I learned through listening to the men gossip, and yes soldiers gossip worse than old women, that the esteemed

Secretary had brought a letter from President Burnet telling the general he had to fight now "because the salvation of the country depended on him doing so." I just rolled my eyes at Hendrick. We both doubted the general would be swayed very much by this letter when he learned our cowardly president was running for the coast.

After lunch, I watched Hendrick head to the general's tent to make his report. Just as he reached the tent's flap, the general stepped out. Unfortunately, I had not been smart enough to distance myself from the general's tent before he emerged and he caught my eye with that penetrating stare of his. I quickly went to work loading supplies on a nearby wagon that was about to be driven onto the Yellowstone, but I could see the general watching me out of the corner of my eye as he listened to Hendrick. Actually, I could feel that sharp gaze upon me, and though I know Hendrick tried to cover for me, deep down I felt the general knew that I had been spying again.

All afternoon I waited to be summoned to the general's tent for my reprimand. I asked Hendrick when he came back from talking with the general if he had asked about the origins of the information. Hendrick informed me he had not asked about that but seemed very interested in the information. For some reason, this did not calm the uneasiness welling up inside me.

We managed to get half of the men, supplies, equipment, and civilians across the river that day. The general seemed pleased with our progress and announced that the rest of us, including himself, would cross tomorrow morning. I wasn't thinking about using that river as a means of transportation, I was thinking about using it for a bathtub. I couldn't even remember the last time I had taken an actual bath. I guess it was when I was working at Mrs. Garcia's tavern before the siege of the Alamo. The Alamo... just the thought made my throat tighten and my eyes smart with tears. I quickly brought my mind back to the prospect of a bath. I wondered around the camp and found a sliver of lye soap that had been thrown out with some wash water. It wasn't a lot, but it would do.

I took my precious sliver of soap and one of my blankets to dry myself off and went down to the river in search of a good place to bathe. I soon found a sandbar behind a wall of yaupon bushes about one hundred yards from camp where the water was shallow enough to spot snakes and other unsavory water creatures. It was perfect. No one from camp could see me. I took off my clothes and lowered myself into the cool water. I don't think anything in my life had ever felt so good. I washed my under garments and laid them out to dry on a rock and then began washing myself. I even caught myself singing hymns I had learned at church as a child. Hunting and fishing with Luke, picking flowers and skipping rocks with Ben and Becky, Christmas dances, skipping Sunday school to spend time with Danny; that life seemed so distant and dreamlike now, and that innocent girl no longer existed. I had changed—whether for better or worse I did not yet know.

15

Tonight General Houston felt very, very tired. Tired from trying to figure out what Santa Anna was going to do and when he should engage El Presidente Pain in the Butt in battle; tired of his men griping and grumbling about retreating when he knew they were no match for Santa Anna's army; tired of the cowardly President Burnet and the rest of the Texian government insisting he fight Santa Anna right now while they were high-tailing it for the coast; tired of being responsible for all the poor displaced civilians who depended on his little army for protection; just so very, very tired. But he had received an interesting piece of information today from Sgt. Hendrick Arnold about Santa Anna. The self-styled Napoleon of the West had separated himself and his army from the other Mexican forces in order to chase down the Texian government headed for Harrisburg. The general had a feeling this could lead to Santa Anna's Waterloo.

But despite his many worries and general weariness, the general couldn't shake his intense curiosity concerning the source of this information. Today, while listening to Arnold's report, he had noticed the young soldier who had spied on Sesma back in camp. He had been wondering where the boy had disappeared to since he had been gone for almost two weeks. In fact, the general realized he hadn't seen the boy since they had left San Felipe de Austin. He thought the boy had deserted after he had upbraided him in front of Smith and Arnold for spying on Sesma, but then the boy just happened to show up in camp today at the same time Arnold arrived with this latest information on Santa Anna. General Houston didn't think it was just a coincidence. He noticed the boy heading for the river after supper, and so, partly to distract his mind and satisfy his curiosity, he decided to follow the boy and confront him concerning his suspicions.

Much to his surprise, General Houston more than satisfied his curiosity. The boy had somewhat of a lead on him, so before he even got to the spot in the bushes where the boy cut through to the river, he heard a female voice singing what sounded like a church hymn. Since he hadn't been to church in quite a few years, he wasn't familiar with the song, but he was definitely sure about the voice singing the song! He peered through the bushes just in time to see a hat being taken off and a cascade of reddish-brown curly hair descend from underneath its wide brim. His eyes widened in astonishment as the reality of what he was seeing hit home: Good Lord! The boy was a young woman!

"Well I'll be!" he said himself. He withdrew from the bushes quickly when he saw her begin to lift her shirt over her head. Then the awkwardness of the situation struck him. Oh Lord, not only was the boy a young woman, but she was bathing in the river not that far from camp, and any of his men could come down here at any moment. Although he figured most of his men were gentlemen and wouldn't invade her privacy by gawking, he wasn't willing to risk giving them the chance to prove it.

General Houston quickly climbed back up the bank to a spot a few yards from where the young woman was bathing, where he could no longer see her behind the bushes but could keep an eye on the bank on either side of her location. He found a big oak tree and sat down with his back against it. What would drive a young woman to disguise herself as a young man and join his army? For that matter, how long had she been with his army without him even knowing it? Since they left Gonzales? If that was so, she must be pretty intelligent and resourceful to keep up the charade that long! Of course, it wasn't as if he didn't have hundreds of other things to keep him occupied besides wondering about the comings and goings of each and every soldier. Hell, he had no idea how many soldiers had deserted over these last few weeks much less when and where this girl had come from.

Oh well, it didn't matter. He would find out soon enough. For a few minutes, he closed his eyes and let his mind empty itself of everything except the sweet, clear notes of her song. Then he pulled out a chunk of wood and his knife from his pocket and began to whittle. He soon felt the tension and worry begin to leave his body and mind as he whittled and listened to the girl sing.

That was where Juan Seguin found the general a little while later. He had been looking for the general to speak with him about his fear of more desertions after tomorrow's crossing if the general continued his retreat toward the Louisiana border. One of his Tejano soldiers said he had seen the general heading for the river, and so Juan had come to find him.

"General—"

"Shhhh."

Juan paused to listen and asked, "Who is she?"

"She's our little spy," Houston said, a smile playing around his lips. It was the first time Juan had seen the general smile since the Alamo fell. "You remember the young boy I told you about that brought the letter back from Sesma's camp? That's him... er...her. I followed him...her out here after supper to confirm my suspicions that she was the one supplying us information about Mexican troop movements and decided after discovering her... er...gender that I had better keep watch at a discrete distance in order to discourage any of our boys from going down to the river."

The general noticed a puzzled look cross Juan's face as the girl ended her song and began to talk aloud to herself. "Oh Danny, things are such a mess without you. I wish you were here to help me figure out what to do."

They both felt a little guilty eavesdropping on the girl's private time, but suddenly, Juan had the feeling he had heard that voice before. Then it hit him, "General, I know her! That's Samantha Autry! She was with her husband, Daniel Autry, at the Alamo. I rode their horse to Gonzales to deliver Travis's message to you."

"Well, well," the general said thoughtfully, then added, "she's been quite a soldier. She's definitely very intelligent and resourceful to have kept us in the dark for this long…and the information she managed to snatch right out from under the Mexican's noses!" He just shook his head and smiled in admiration. Then sympathetically, he mused, "I bet that young girl has been through hell. I'll be as gentle as possible when I tell her she has to go with the civilians when the fighting starts."

"Sir," said Juan, "she is a tough one. I watched her work and fight alongside her husband the entire time we were in the Alamo. Now that Danny is dead, she is probably out for revenge. I'm pretty sure she won't go willingly."

"I hear her getting dressed. Let's head back to camp. Hopefully on the way back, I will figure out what to say to her."

"Good luck, General."

16

The water felt so good, I was tempted to just stay in it just floating on my back and thinking of home and Danny while the flood of tears continually coursed down my cheeks. As I fingered the gold locket Danny had given me at the Alamo, I caught myself speaking softly to the darkness, "Oh Danny, things are such a mess without you. I wish you were here to help me figure out what to do."

I closed my eyes and just floated in the water until my fingers and toes began to shrivel. I reluctantly forced myself to get out of the water and get dressed. My undergarments were still damp, but at least they were clean. As I dressed, I wondered what awaited me back at camp. I was sure the general had figured out by now that it was me that had given the information to Hendrick. With a deep sigh and one last long look at that peaceful river, I climbed the bank and headed back to camp.

Sure enough, I had no sooner reached its outskirts when Juan Seguin met me with news that the general wanted to see me. I made sure that my hat was planted solidly over my hair and followed him to the general's tent.

The general had been sitting on a wooden crate, but stood up when I entered. I was struck once more by how tall he was. He towered above me, and those piercing blue eyes seemed to bore right through me. I met his gaze only briefly before I found myself staring at my feet.

"General, you wish to see me?" I asked and quickly cleared my throat to hide my quivering voice.

"Yes, I do, Private Sam, or should I say Samantha Autry?"

My eyes snapped up to meet his as he gently pulled my hat from my head. My hair had grown back quite a bit. It had always grown fast, and now it tumbled down around my face. I just stared up at him in astonishment and fear at being discovered.

"H-H-How did you find out?" I managed to ask in my still quivering voice.

"I followed you down to the river with the intention of questioning you about the information Sergeant Arnold reported to me today and saw you remove your hat. When I realized who you were and what you were about to do, I, of course, withdrew to a location from which I could not see but could hear you in order to ensure none of the men found you. A short time later, Captain Seguin came along to find me and identified you. You really need to be more careful if you intend to…er…go for more swims in the future."

I glanced at Juan and saw the chagrined look on his face. I really couldn't blame him. Recognizing me probably had surprised him as much as it had surprised the general. He probably thought he would never see anyone from the Alamo again.

"Would you care to explain, Private?" the general inquired gently.

Right then it hit me…I had been caught…there was no reason to be cautious or hide the truth any longer. I felt my jaw set as I raised my head and stuck out my chin like I used to do when Pa or Danny would forbid me to do something I felt I needed to do.

"Yes, sir," I answered quietly, looking him squarely in the eyes. "I am here because I want to make Santa Anna pay for what he did to my friends and my Danny at the Alamo."

"I see," said the general quietly as he continued to gaze at me. "And I suppose you will want to be in the fight when we finally engage Santa Anna's army." He crossed his arms and sighed heavily. "I understand your desire to avenge the death of your friends and your husband, but you must know that I cannot allow a young woman such as yourself to be placed in such dangerous circumstances. I have no choice but to ensure that you accompany the civilians out of harms' way when the time comes. I do want you to know that I greatly appreciate all of your assistance. You managed to obtain very valuable information from the Mexicans, although God alone knows how you did it. That is all. You are dismissed." Then he turned back to the map he was studying on the crate in front of him.

I glanced at Juan as my chin began to quiver with anger and my eyes filled with tears. "With all due respect, sir, I will not be dismissed!"

The general's head snapped up from his map. Then he slowly turned around on his crate and stared at me with those stern blue eyes. Finally he asked in a deadly calm voice, "What did you say, Mrs. Autry?"

"I said I will not be dismissed! I will not be dismissed ever again! Except for my home town, you and everybody else in Texas dismissed me and everyone else in the Alamo to…to the… cruelty and barbarism of Santa Anna and his army of butchers! None of you came to help! Not one of you! And you have the nerve to tell me I'm dismissed?! That morning I did my best to help Danny by loading his spare rifles during that battle, and while I was doing so, I saw Colonel Travis fall off the north wall with a bullet through his forehead! I watched Santa Anna's men shoot Juan's friends as they tried to reload their cannon on the west wall and bayonet their bodies until they were unrecognizable. Enrique Esparza ran out screaming for his father, and I had just convinced him to go back to his mother when a flood of Mexicans breached every wall. I watched Colonel Crockett and his men club Mexicans with their rifles because they didn't have time to reload until they were overpowered and bayonetted to death. One of his men, Danny's Uncle Micajah, died in my arms."

By this time my tears were blinding me, but I couldn't stop. It felt like a huge wall was crumbling inside me and all the pain and anger I had kept bottled up came bursting forth, flooding my heart and overwhelming my senses until all I could see or hear were the images and sounds from that horrible day. My sobs shook my body and choked me so that I could barely speak, but I felt if I didn't, the pain would so totally engulf me that I would cease to exist. "I heard the shots fired in the baptistery when they killed Colonel Bowie. The entire compound was nothing but screaming and yelling, and cannon fire and rifle fire splitting the blackness, and thousands of Mexican soldiers emerging from the smoke and darkness with bayonets jabbing, and eyes glowing with hatred!"

As I relived the events of that day, every terrible moment flashing before my eyes blinded me to the fact that the stern, battle-hardened General Houston had taken me into his arms and was holding me gently. All I could see was that Mexican soldier coming for Danny. "Then this Mexican soldier just appeared out of the smoke and darkness like a demon from hell and shot my Danny. I tried to shoot him but someone hit me over the head."

By this time, the flood began to ebb and my sobbing began to quiet. In a small, exhausted voice I continued, "The next thing I knew, I was kneeling in front of Santa Anna with my hands tied behind my back. He wanted me to beg for my life, but I told him to just go ahead and kill me. He wouldn't do it, so I told him he would regret letting me live."

The general held me until my crying stopped and I could stand on my own. Then he turned his back to me hoping, I knew, that I wouldn't see him wipe his eyes with the back of his hand. I heard Juan sniff and turned to see him wipe tears from his eyes also. I felt bad about being the one to tell him about his friends.

I looked at the floor and then looked back up at the general. "I apologize for that outburst, sir. That was very disrespectful and should never have happened. I don't know what's wrong with me. I don't normally behave this way. I understand you are just trying to do what is best for me. But, sir, if I can help you in any way, I want to do so…for Danny, for all the men in the Alamo, for you, for Texas."

"All right, Samantha, all right," he answered in a voice rough with emotion. "You have my permission to keep your disguise and help out where you can. But I'm ordering you to camp with the civilians and *stay out of the fighting*."

17

The next day the rest of the army crossed the Brazos and we continued marching eastward. I kept my disguise but stayed with the civilians as I had been commanded. It didn't really matter to me since there was nothing really going on except the seemingly endless retreating. I did wonder if Santa Anna had managed to capture the Texian government at Harrisburg. I hate to admit it but a small part of me hoped he had. I was angry with President Burnet and the rest of our so-called leaders for running away like little girls and for giving the general such a hard time. I learned later that the government did barely manage to escape in a small boat headed to Galveston, which enraged El Diablo Presidente so much that he burned down Harrisburg. Harrisburg. Little did I know that the next day, Harrisburg would become the denouement of the first chapter in the Republic of Texas's story.

All I knew at that moment was that I felt so very much better! I knew I would probably mourn for Danny and my friends at the Alamo for a very long time. But the bottled-up pain and anger that had caused my stomach to tie itself into knots seemed to be gone. I felt like I could breathe again, I could laugh again, and best of all, I didn't have to worry that much about keeping my identity a secret. Oh, I remained in disguise when I worked around the other men. But I figured since the general and Juan knew about me, I could relax a little. I wanted to tell Hendrick, but the general continually sent all the scouts out on spy missions to monitor Santa Anna's movements and I never got the chance. I kind of envied them. Secretly, I think I enjoyed spying. Spying had provided me with brief periods of feeling alive during a time when, for the most part, I felt dead.

It was really nice to finally be able to talk to Juan. We talked long into the night after my outburst in the general's tent. He wanted to know about the last days at the Alamo and how his friends felt about him leaving. I assured him that from what I could understand of their conversation after he left, they understood that he had to try to get help for the Alamo and just hoped he had gotten through the Mexican lines. One thing I knew for certain, General Houston would always have my unswerving loyalty for showing me such kindness and understanding, and Santa Anna my contempt, hatred, and hopefully soon, my revenge.

I will never forget that day, Friday, April 15, 1836. The day before the general had held a very intense meeting with Secretary of War Rusk and several other officers about whether we should go to Harrisburg or keep retreating east to the Louisiana border to hopefully recruit at least five thousand more volunteers. The reason I knew about the meeting was because I eavesdropped outside his tent. I was becoming quite the expert at spying, even though the general almost caught me sneaking around the back of his tent when he came out of the meeting. Actually, I think he saw me but he didn't say anything. Anyway, from what I could gather from the meeting, no conclusive decision was made, so we kept marching east.

The weather turned bad that day with a steady downpour of rain. We had a heck of a time sloshing through the mud and trying to keep the twin sisters from getting stuck. It took ten of us pulling on ropes and pushing from behind to keep the sisters moving. Once the general rode by and saw me pulling on one of the ropes. He didn't say a word but gave me a look that at one time would have frozen my very soul. Now I just smiled, saluted, and went back to work. He had told me I could help, and by golly, I was doing just that! Finally, we came to a farm owned by a kindly lady named Mrs. Mann. She took pity on us and loaned us a team of her oxen to haul the sisters. We were extremely grateful for her generosity.

For two and a half days, we slogged and sloshed our way eastward. We finally reached a fork in the road near Abram Roberts' farm which was marked by a strange looking tree with gnarled, twisted branches. This tree became known as the which-way tree because it was at this tree that the general finally made the decision that would decide the fate of Texas. The right-hand fork would take us to Harrisburg and Santa Anna; the left, further east to Nacogdoches and eventually the Louisiana border. Mr. Roberts was standing on his gate yelling, "That right hand road will take you to Harrisburg." We all held our breath as we watched the general approach the tree and that fateful fork in the road. Then he gave the order. "Columns, right!" A loud cheer erupted among the ranks! We were on our way fight Santa Anna!

Although the main part of the army took the right hand road, the general ordered Wylie Martin to escort the civilians to Nacogdoches instead of following the army. I found out about this when Juan requested to speak with me during our dinner break.

"Samantha, I hate to be the bearer of bad news, but the general has sent me to tell you that you will have to go with the rest of the civilians to Nacogdoches."

I just gave him a blank, uncomprehending stare. "What?"

"The general wants you to go with the civilians," Juan repeated, slightly impatiently.

"Well, Captain Seguin, if the general wants me to go with the civilians, he needs to come and tell me himself!" I retorted.

"Samantha, please be reasonable. The general has a lot to deal with right now, and you knew you wouldn't be allowed in the fight. He told you so the other night."

Tears welled up in my eyes as I gave Juan a long, beseeching look. I saw sympathy, but also firm resolve. "Very well," I said looking dejectedly at the ground. "I'll go join the women and children." I picked up my pack and headed over to the civilian camp. I found a woman, Mrs. Taylor, who was trying to corral her children and pack her family's belongings all at the same time. I was playing with the children while she packed when suddenly a commotion broke out near the twin sisters which demanded Juan's attention. As soon as he left to see what was going on and Mrs. Taylor had everything packed, I crammed my hat back on my head, picked up my pack and rifle, and headed back to my unit. Go with the civilians my hind leg! It would be a cold day in hell before *that* would happen.

I soon discovered the source of the commotion when I got back to camp. Mrs. Mann had returned and she was *not* happy. It turned out she thought her darling oxen were going to pull civilian wagons to Nacogdoches, not cannon into battle. You could hear her all through the camp.

"General Houston, you lied to me. You said those oxen were going to Nacogdoches."

"Mrs. Mann, please, I apologize for the misunderstanding, but we desperately need your oxen to haul our artillery."

"I'm sorry, General Houston, but I want my oxen."

"Well, Mrs. Mann, we cannot spare them."

That seemed to be the wrong answer for Mrs. Mann. I heard her reply, "I don't care about your cannon, I want my oxen!" And with that, she pulled out a Bowie knife, cut her oxen free, and walked off leading the desperately needed animals behind her. Our wagon master, Mr. Rohrer, decided to go after her and get the oxen even though the general warned him against this. He returned to camp that evening with his shirt cut to shreds and no oxen. Even though I knew it would be tough going without the oxen, I couldn't help laughing.

I didn't laugh for long. The rain continued to fall and the road became one long, continuous muddy mess. Every step was a battle, as we sunk to our knees in mud. We didn't stop to rest or cook anything and ate jerky or cold biscuits or whatever we could eat without stopping. Finally, after two and a half days and fifty-five miles of muddy road, we made it to Harrisburg only to find it burned to the ground. It didn't matter. The Texian Army would run no more.

18

That same day, Deaf Smith, Captain Karnes, and Hendrick captured a Mexican courier carrying letters addressed to Santa Anna. He also had Colonel Travis's saddlebags, so I knew he had been at the Alamo, and I felt that little flame of anger begin to kindle inside of me. The letters stated that El Diablo Presidente was at New Washington with a small force just a few miles from Harrisburg. The general knew he had him just where he wanted him. All we had to do was cross Buffalo Bayou and catch him.

We spent most of the day, April 19, crossing the bayou on an old raft and a leaking boat. We finally made it and thought we might get to rest, but the general ordered us to keep marching. We marched until midnight and everybody was so very tired, the general was forced to call a halt. Most of us just lay down wherever we could and fell asleep.

The next morning, Deaf and his boys came galloping into camp shouting that Santa Anna had burned New Washington and was headed to Lynchburg. We knew then there would be no breakfast. Cussing and griping, the men packed up and we headed for Lynchburg. Missing breakfast proved worth it. We beat the Mexicans there and were able to find a perfect position to attack the Mexicans among a thick grove of oak trees. As if to prove even further that our fortune had changed for the better, some of the boys captured a Mexican flatboat carrying food and supplies for Santa Anna's army. We finally got our breakfast, courtesy of El Diablo Presidente himself!

After I finished eating and while the rest of the camp was finishing up, I decided to explore our surroundings. Oak trees lined the bank of Buffalo Bayou, but thinned out the further I walked from the bank, surrendering to grassy areas that eventually bottomed out into marshes bordering the San Jacinto River. It was then that I saw the Mexicans setting up camp just to the east of our position! I ran back to camp to inform the general only to discover that Deaf Smith and his scouts had already reported all the details of the Mexican troop movements. Word spread quickly throughout the camp, and everyone knew by the end of the day that it was only a matter of time before the battle would begin.

Unfortunately for the general, the battle almost began before he wanted it to. The next day, right after breakfast, I was helping Colonel Neill and his men set up some artillery positions just behind the stand of oaks where we had made camp when a squadron of Mexican dragoons appeared over a small rise just in front of our position.

I heard one of the men yell, "The Mexicans are upon us!"

Colonel Neill responded immediately, "Load the cannon, boys," and soon the twin sisters roared to life. The Mexican dragoons retreated before the fury of the sisters, but now that the Mexicans had ascertained our location, they began firing their cannon. The cannon battle didn't last long, however, because Santa Anna had picked such a terrible place to set up camp. The twins soon took out some mules, a soldado or two, and destroyed several of the Mexican bulwarks. The Mexican cannon soon ceased firing, and a long silence followed as cannon smoke billowed across the field and eventually evaporated in the morning breeze.

I thought we had gotten through the skirmish unscathed until I heard Colonel Neill moan in pain. He had been wounded by scattering grapeshot from the Mexican cannon fire. I ran over to help Colonel Neill and did my best to staunch the bleeding from his wounds until Dr. Labadie could take over. As I headed back to my artillery post, I heard Colonel Sidney Sherman yelling to his cavalry, "C'mon, boys, let's finish 'em off!"

The general roared, "Damn it, Sherman, hold your position!"

Sherman refused and insisted on pressing our advantage. The general reluctantly gave him permission to go only on a reconnaissance mission to ascertain the damage sustained by the Mexicans. This, of course, didn't satisfy Sherman and he led his cavalry unit in a full-scale attack against the Mexican cavalry. Unfortunately for Sherman, the Mexican cavalry were much better trained. The Mexicans charged Sherman's men with their lances while they struggled to reload their rifles. I saw Secretary of War Rusk who had joined up with Sherman's unit get knocked off his horse, and watched in horror as Mexican lancers surrounded him.

Just when I thought he was a goner for sure, a Texian soldier riding a big white stallion charged across the field and killed two of the Mexican lancers causing the rest to scatter and saving Rusk's life. It was Private Mirabeau B. Lamar, and, believe me, I had never seen such an expert horse rider in all my days!

Then, just to add a little more gut wrenching excitement to the general's day, Lieutenant Billingsley ordered his men to charge out to rescue Sherman's men. I thought the general's head would explode. His face became beet red as he yelled, "Billingsley, I order you to countermarch this instant!"

I heard Billingsley tell the general, "Countermarch yourself," as he foolishly led his men out to assist Sherman. By then, Sherman and his men began to retreat back to the woods with Billingsley following. My heart pounded nervously hoping and praying they made it back to the woods with no more injuries.

But Private Mirabeau B. Lamar got the chance to be a hero once more. Just when I thought everyone would make it back to the safety of the woods, a Mexican cavalryman knocked one of our men off his horse. It turned out to be Private Walter Lane, one of our youngest soldiers. As he struggled to get up, several Mexican lancers rode toward him, their menacing spears aimed straight for the boy!

Just then Private Lamar galloped in between Lane and the Mexican lancers, shielding him from their spears and shooting one soldado with his pistol. Then Captain Karnes galloped up behind him and pulled Walter up onto his horse. I watched in amazement as Santa Anna's dragoons actually began applauding for Lamar and Karnes as they galloped back toward our camp. Private Lamar turned his horse around, and with a contemptuous grin, bowed toward the Mexican army. I also couldn't help laughing out loud as Santa Anna threw a tantrum, furiously yelling and waving his arms around.

Santa Anna wasn't the only furious general on the battlefield that day. Despite Lamar's heroics, General Houston was fit to be tied. The Mexicans had won this round, but luckily this little skirmish had only cost us two wounded men. I knew what the general was thinking. With our numbers and the fact that Santa Anna could receive reinforcements at any time, we had only one good fight in us. Any more episodes like this could cost us the war.

19

So far I had managed to stay out of the general's sight and felt pretty sure he thought I had followed the civilians to Nacogdoches. After all, he had a lot more important things on his mind than concerning himself with a foolish sixteen-year-old kid. But after the events of today, I had the feeling that tomorrow might prove a pivotal day in the fight for Texas, and I knew that decision time was upon me. Should I take part in the battle that would probably take place tomorrow, and most likely be discovered by the general or Juan, or should I just stay in the background as much as possible? I lay awake for quite a while thinking about this and finally during the wee hours of the morning, I made up my mind. If we fought today, I was going to be in the middle of it. I owed it to Danny. If I lived, I would just suffer the consequences, and I figured if the general had anything to do with it, there would be some serious consequences.

I was not the only one sleep eluded that night. I could see the General's tent from my little camping spot. I noticed lantern light burning within its confines when I fell asleep, so I knew that the general had been awake well after I had finally fallen asleep. It seemed I had only just closed my eyes when our 4:00 a.m. wakeup call forced me out of a fitful sleep.

I reluctantly rolled out of my blankets and began rekindling my little fire to make some coffee and cook a little bite of breakfast.

As soon as I sat up, I had second thoughts about breakfast. My stomach felt queasy. I sat there, hoping the feeling would go away, but the smell of frying meat wafting through the air from other campfires just made me feel worse. Finally, I had to make a dash for the edge of the woods, or I would have made everyone else sick. After this I felt a lot better, and so I ate some biscuits and drank a little coffee. My nerves were definitely getting the better of me.

By nine, the general still had not gotten up and the men were getting angry. I heard men asking very loudly if the "Big Drunk" intended to sleep all day. In the general's defense, I knew he hadn't slept much at all since leaving Groces' Plantation and really didn't blame him for sleeping in a while. It did make me wonder if he planned to attack Santa Anna today, or wait for El Presidente to do the attacking.

I didn't have long to wait for an answer. Around ten Deaf Smith rode into camp with news that General Cos had arrived with 540 men to reinforce Santa Anna. Now we no longer had a numerical advantage over the Mexicans and my stomach did another flip flop. The general emerged from his tent when Deaf rode into camp and ordered him to follow him inside. When Deaf emerged I watched him, Hendrick, and Captain Karnes ride off toward Vince's Bridge behind us on Vince's Bayou. Then several of the officers including Secretary of War Rusk forced their way into the general's tent demanding a meeting. By this time it was noon, and I knew everyone was getting very antsy wondering if we were going to fight today. I could hear their angry voices carrying throughout the camp, so I knew the rest of the men heard also.

"General, we have to attack now. Cos has already arrived to reinforce Santa Anna and Filisola is probably right behind!"

"We're gonna lose our advantage if we don't attack now!"

"That's right! General, we have no other choice!"

"Yes, we do. We can let Santa Anna attack! We have the tactical advantage here in this tree grove."

"That's true. Maybe we should wait for the Mexicans to attack!"

"No…Yes…No."

Then distinct comments became lost in an incoherent babble of voices. Finally, the general just dismissed them without a word.

I did some quick calculations in my head. We had around 912 men and Santa Anna now had, oh probably, around 1,200. The odds were no longer in our favor, but believe me, I would take these odds over the ones we had had at the Alamo any day!

We all went back to sitting around and waiting…and waiting…and waiting. The tension invading the camp seemed physically palpable. Finally, at about three thirty that afternoon, the general emerged from his tent and ordered everyone to line up in battle formation. The general had bought a big white stallion from a friend's wife on the road to Harrisburg. He now mounted that magnificent animal and rode back and forth in front us as he gave us our battle speech.

"Gentlemen, today we are going to meet the enemy. Some of us may be killed, but those of us who survive will remember this day and this battle as long as we live. For today…remember the Alamo! Remember Goliad! And give them hell!" A yell went up from the ranks, and I could see the fire begin to burn in everyone's eyes.

We loaded our rifles and formed into two parallel lines with the twin sisters in the middle and the cavalry on the left. To tell you the truth, I still didn't know what I was going to do, so I finally just decided to line up with Juan's Tejanos who had joined Colonel Sherman's men. Because of Sherman's actions from the day before, the general had relieved Colonel Sherman of command of the cavalry, had promoted Lamar, and given him command of the cavalry. I definitely agreed with this action. Mirabeau Lamar had proven himself to be a heck of a horseman and a very brave man.

Then I heard the general order Juan and his company to guard the camp because he was afraid they would be mistaken for Santa Anna's soldados during the chaos of battle. But I couldn't help smiling with pride-filled satisfaction when Juan presented the general with an argument he couldn't possibly refute: "General, this is our fight also. We have nowhere to go if Santa Anna conquers Texas." So the general ordered them to fight with Sherman's men and to put cards in their hats to distinguish them from Santa Anna's men. As Juan saluted and turned to go, I saw a small smile of pride cross the general's usually stern countenance. I put a card in my hat and got in line with Juan's company. My heart began to pound in my chest as the realization hit that we were really going to fight the Santanistas.

Just before we began to forward march, Deaf Smith and his men rode up beside us. Deaf yelled, "Vince's Bridge is down, boys, fight for your lives! We had a little four-piece band, and the only song they knew was a love song called 'Will You Come to the Bower?'" I thought the song was a little scandalous, but, oh well.

Then everything seemed to happen at once. The twin sisters let out a defiant roar as they smashed the Mexican camp with cannon balls filled with grapeshot. Colonel Lamar gave the order for his cavalry to charge, and the general ordered the rest of us to march. He finally called a halt about halfway to the Mexican camp and ordered us to fire. The afternoon air exploded with the deafening roar of gunfire as all of our rifles fired simultaneously. Then the general tried to stop our line so that we could reload, but most of the men were afraid our lines would be cut to pieces by the Mexicans. Secretary of War Rusk galloped ahead yelling, "Don't stop now, boys! Go ahead! Give 'em hell!" Everyone just started running toward the Mexican camp.

I was expecting to meet a wall of gun fire from the Mexicans, but the strange thing was, we had taken them completely by surprise! They weren't expecting us! In fact, as far as I could tell, many of them, including El Presidente, had been taking a siesta! It was unbelievable! Our men ran completely over their bulwarks and began to club any Mexican they saw to death, yelling, "Remember the Alamo! Remember Goliad!" Some of the Mexican generals tried to organize their men to fight back, but didn't have time to do so. Some of the soldados managed to load their rifles and would stop and fire. But they were easy to pick out and kill because the rest of the Mexican soldados were running away like scared chickens.

The Mexican generals weren't the only ones who lost control of their men. The Texian lines had disintegrated into small frenzied groups driven by anger and vengeance, and there was no way the general could get their attention long enough to reorganize them. They clubbed the Mexicans with such fury, that those who escaped the clubbing just turned and ran. But that didn't stop the Texians. They chased them down until they caught them and then proceeded to club them to death. I heard Mexicans screaming "Me no Alamo, Me no Goliad," but to no avail.

The sight of all that carnage took me completely by surprise. I hesitated momentarily, and that's when I saw the general's horse go down with a lethal gunshot wound. I didn't realize it at the time, and I don't think the general did either, but he was wounded also. I saw a Mexican horse running lose without a rider, and ran after him trying to grab his reins. At that very moment, a soldado ran between me and the horse. I froze for a split second when I saw the soldado reach in his belt for his pistol, and that's when the strangest event of my life occurred.

My mind seemed to stay frozen as my eyes locked with his, but my body began reacting on its own. I became aware that my arms had lifted Danny's rifle, and with my eyes still fixed steadily on the soldado, they swung the rifle striking the man on the side of the head. The soldado seemed to fall in slow motion as my eyes traveled from the blank look on his face to the horse's reins behind him. Then my mind regained control of my body, and I grabbed the reins and ran toward the general.

The general was frantically looking around for a new mount when I ran up with the horse. "General, over here," I shouted and then realized that this was probably a big mistake. The general recognized me. I could tell by the angry look he gave me as he got to his feet.

"Samantha Autry!" he yelled, gritting his teeth in anger.

"General, just take the horse!" I shouted in exasperation.

He gave me one more furious look, jumped on the horse, and rode toward his men, who by now had chased most of the Mexicans into Peggy Lake where they continued the massacre. I ran after him toward the lake and wished I hadn't once I got there. The sun shining warmly on the calm surface of the middle of the lake seemed to belie the bloody chaos churning near its shoreline. Even as the soldados floundered in the water without a weapon wanting only to surrender or escape, the Texians continued to club and shoot them. I saw that lake turn from dirty brown to red in a matter of minutes. Even though there was definitely no love lost between Santa Anna's army and myself, watching my fellow Texians massacre them made me sick. I saw the general riding desperately along the bank yelling for the men to stop the killing, but it did no good. Although the killing seemed to go on forever, the entire battle lasted only eighteen minutes. Vengeance belonged to the Texian army that day.

While the general endeavored to stop the carnage that was occurring on Peggy Lake, a terrible thought struck me. I had not seen El Presidente one time during the entire battle. Where was that coward? I figured the general would want to take him prisoner, even though if it was left up to me, I would most likely kill him. I found another stray horse, jumped on its back and headed back to the Mexican camp. It was a good thing I did, because I arrived just in time to see El Diablo Presidente change into a dead Mexican private's shirt, mount a horse, and disappear toward Vince's Bayou probably thinking he was going to get to cross Vince's Bridge. Unfortunately for El Diablo Presidente, he didn't know we had burned Vince's Bridge.

As I kicked the horse into a gallop, I felt something hit my upper right arm just below the shoulder. I remained too focused on following Santa Anna to pay much attention to it at the time, but as I continued to ride, my arm began to hurt pretty badly. I felt something warm and wet running down and dripping from my elbow. I took my eyes off El Presidente for just a moment to glance at my arm. I was bleeding. I had been shot, but I couldn't stop to tend to it now and risk losing El Presidente.

I continued to follow Santa Anna until I was certain he was heading for the bayou. He heard my horse crashing through the brush, and stupidly jumped off his horse to hide in the tall grass by the bayou. The horse took off running leaving poor, poor El Presidente stranded! The idea to take him myself crossed my mind, but I had no rifle or pistol, and I figured Santa Anna's pride wouldn't allow him to be captured by a kid. The sun began its descent into the west as I continued to quietly stalk El Presidente along the bank and weigh my options. I didn't figure Santa Anna would get far tonight, especially since he had no bridge to cross. He was probably thinking Urrea or Filisola would find him there tomorrow or the next day since they were probably on their way with reinforcements. Most likely, he would find a relatively dry spot along the bayou's bank to camp for the night and wait. I had managed to stay out of his line of sight, so I decided to return to camp and report his whereabouts to the general. I figured I had nothing to lose since I was already in trouble with the general, and I knew he would be pretty anxious to know the whereabouts of Santa Anna.

As I rode, I began to feel lightheaded. My arm was still bleeding pretty heavily, so I stopped just long enough to tear off my shirt sleeve and bind it around my arm. That seemed to slow the bleeding somewhat, but I knew I needed to hurry if I was going to make it back to camp in some sort of conscious, coherent state. So I nudged the horse into a gallop and raced back to camp.

I did make it back, just barely. I saw Juan run toward me through a foggy haze with a concerned expression on his face. He caught me in his arms just as I fell off my horse.

"Samantha, mi amiga, what are you doing here? What happened?"

"I'll explain...later," I managed to reply. "Need to see the general. Santa Anna...down by Vince's Bayou."

"Let's get that arm looked at first."

"No...no. The general...needs to know."

Juan sighed heavily and gave me a reproachful look. "Can you walk?"

"Yes...if you help me a little."

Actually, he had to help me a lot. Juan led me over to a huge oak tree under which the general lay on his old saddle blanket with his right foot bandaged and propped up on his saddle. He must have been in a lot of pain because as I approached him, he was murmuring, "Where is Santa Anna?" Then he cried out "All is lost, all is lost!"

With Juan's help, I half knelt and half fell down beside him. "General, General," I said soothingly. "It's okay. Santa Anna is down by Vince's Bridge. He's dressed as a private and I figure he's waiting on Filsola or Urrea. All you have to do is send some men to get him."

The general propped himself up on his elbows. Gradually his eyes began to focus as he stared at my face. "Samantha, my little Sam?"

"Yes, sir," I answered. "I'm right here." And then unconsciousness overtook me.

When I awoke the next morning, I found myself lying on the saddle blanket next to the general. My arm throbbed painfully, but it was covered with a clean bandage and Dr. Labadie assured me that it was a clean wound. Evidently the musket ball had gone all the way through my arm, so he needed only to sew it up. The general kept looking down at me with a worried expression on his face, so I finally decided to prop myself up against the tree to assure him that I was going to live. Of course, once he saw that I could sit up okay, he began lecturing me about orders and that

I could be tried and court martialed for disobedience. It was like being at home listening to Pa when I got into trouble. I just rolled my eyes, and answered, "Yes, sir," every now and then. I didn't even understand what he was talking about most of the time.

Just then, Major Forbes and Chief of Staff Hockley came toward us dragging what looked to be a Mexican private. They passed the area where we were keeping Mexican prisoners, and as they passed I heard some of the prisoners begin to say "El Presidente, El Presidente." Evidently the general had sent some men to pick up El Diablo early this morning, because here he was in the flesh.

I quickly found my hat lying next to me and put it on stuffing my hair under it pulling it low over my face. The general gave me a quizzical look, but didn't say anything. I just gazed calmly at Santa Anna as he approached the general and didn't say a word.

The men found a box on which El Presidente could sit, and brought Colonel Almonte to translate. As soon as he figured out that he wouldn't be shot on the spot, he began his surrender by making obnoxious grandiose remarks concerning himself. "The conqueror of the Napoleon of the West is born to no common destiny. He can afford to be generous to the vanquished."

And that's when I lost my temper. I sat up straight, "Generous to the vanquished!" I snapped. "Oh, like you were so very generous at the Alamo, you sorry son of Satan—" I didn't finish what I wanted to say because Ma's reproving face suddenly appeared in my mind. The general laid a hand on my arm to calm me down.

"You should have remembered that, sir, at the Alamo," the general finished for me in a much more professional tone. Then the general did an odd thing. He just sat there giving Santa Anna that cold, calculating, stare that had intimidated me so many times before. Santa Anna shifted uncomfortably on his box and then stared at the ground.

The general continued to give him that cold, impenetrable stare for a few more minutes, then he looked at me and asked,

"Well, Little Sam, what shall we do with the magnificent Napoleon of the West?"

I looked at him in surprise wondering what he had planned. His eyes glinted with amusement as he winked at me and gestured toward his pistol lying on the blanket by his side. Suddenly I understood. Slowly I stood up and took off my hat. My hair fell around my face and down my back in a cascade of curls. Santa Anna and the rest of the men standing around gasped.

I caught Hendrick's eyes as he stood guard behind Santa Anna. He had just walked up behind Santa Anna and now stared at me with a shocked expression. Then giving me that boyish, easygoing grin of his, he exclaimed "Well, I'll be danged! Don't that beat all!"

I grabbed the general's pistol which had been lying on the blanket and slowly walked over to Santa Anna. Though I figured it would never happen, I had dreamed about this day for almost two months. I pointed the pistol at his temple and cocked the hammer back. Then I bent down and spoke softly in his ear, *"Le dije usted lo lamentaria me permite vivir*...I told you, you would regret letting me live." As the look of surprise and recognition crossed his face, I pulled the trigger.

EPILOGUE

Of course, nothing happened except that El Diablo Presidente wet his fancy britches. The general and I both knew that pistol wasn't loaded because the firing cap was missing. "Now El Diablo Presidente, I want you and the rest of your armies to get out of my Texas," I stated boldly.

"I agree," the general said. "The terms of your surrender will be these: You will order all of your armies to leave Texas immediately. Then you will sign over any and all claims that Mexico possesses to Texas to the Texian government. If you refuse these terms, I will probably give Samantha a loaded pistol."

A very loud cheer went up from the men as Santa Anna agreed to the terms. After all, he had lost 630 men that day and we had only lost nine. Santa Anna did sign over all rights to Texas and ordered his armies to retreat back across the Rio Grande. The Republic of Texas was born.

And so my brief profession as a spy ended with the conclusion of the Texas Revolution. My life after this became pretty mundane. I returned home to live in mine and Danny's little house in Gonzales. It was still there just as we had left it last January when we went to San Antonio four months ago. So much had happened during that time that it really seemed like ages ago. Anyway, I cleaned up the house and planted a small garden. I found the rest of the silver Danny and I had brought from Tennessee still hidden in the cellar, so I used some of it to buy a milk cow and a new rifle for hunting and protection. The general sent me an army discharge letter for exemplary service in the cause of Texas independence and a small stipend for my service. The letter meant the most, of course. Everything was going pretty well, except for missing Danny so much.

I had only one problem. Every morning, I woke up with that queasy feeling I had first experienced that morning before the Battle of San Jacinto as it came to be known. Sometimes I would be sick, but sometimes I could eat a piece of bread and the queasiness would go away. I also noticed my dresses were becoming tight around the middle, which I at first attributed to finally being able to eat regularly. But one morning it occurred to me that even though I was eating regularly and the rest of my life seemed back to normal, my body was not. Then a shocking thought struck me! No, that couldn't be it! I started counting back to the last time Danny and I were together before we went into the Alamo and it added up. I went into town to see the doctor and he confirmed my suspicions. I was almost three months pregnant. I was going to have Danny's baby!

I finally wrote to my family to let them know that I was still alive and my good news. I also wrote to Danny's parents to let them know about Danny. That was a very difficult letter to write, and I was glad I also had the good news about the baby to share with them. After receiving my letters detailing the events of the war and how rich the land was in Texas, my brother, Luke, and his wife, Rachel, decided to move here. They bought half of my land and some land adjacent, and lived with me while they built their house. It was very nice to have their company and help, especially since I was pregnant.

Danielle Autry came into the world on November 24, 1836. She had Danny's blue eyes and black hair. Unfortunately, she inherited my unruly curls and temper, but she was a beautiful baby! Danny would have been so proud. As I held my daughter for the very first time, I knew he was in heaven smiling at the sight of his beautiful daughter. For the first time in a very long time, I felt at peace.

The next year, Ma, Pa, Becky, and Ben also moved to Texas. I don't think I have ever been happier in my life to see my family, especially my Ma and Pa. I guess I hadn't had the time to realize how very much I had missed them. Luckily for me, they were too glad to see me and especially Danielle to remember to be upset with me for running away to Texas. Sadly, Grandma and Grandpa had passed away last winter from cholera, but Elizabeth was happily married to a Tennessee state representative and now lived in Nashville, Tennessee.

In February of that year, I received a special, yet poignant letter from Lt. Col. Juan Seguin, who was now commander of San Antonio's military force. He was writing to invite me to a special burial ceremony for the defenders of the Alamo who had been cremated by Santa Anna's men that fateful, awful morning. It had always bothered me that Danny had never had a proper burial. There would never by a grave for Danielle and I to visit. Except for Danielle, there was nothing left of Danny except my memories. I knew it would be difficult, but I knew I needed to go.

I arrived at San Fernando Cathedral just as a priest was performing the last rites ceremony over a small coffin containing the men's ashes that had been gathered at the Alamo. My eyes filled with tears at the site of that little box. It occurred to me how ironic it was that that small box whose purpose was to bury the dead only succeeded in resurrecting a flood of memories for me. After the rites were read, Juan asked if there were any present who had been at the Alamo when it fell. I stood with Danielle and walked up to join him at the front of the church. When he saw us, Juan's eyes filled with tears as he first gave me a hug and then took Danielle into his arms. He then requested that the military, followed by city dignitaries, family members, and the rest of the citizenry line up for a processional to carry the box back to the Alamo for an honorary eulogy. Carrying Danielle and with me walking by his side, Juan led the processional back at the Alamo, where he gave a very moving speech honoring its defenders. Although the ceremony was emotionally difficult, I finally felt that I had had my chance to tell my friends at the Alamo good-bye.

I stayed in San Antonio a few more days and visited with Juan and his family and reacquainted myself with the city. San Antonio was growing rapidly as was the rest of Texas, but it continued to retain its old world beauty and charm. I thought about going back to the Alamo one last time before I returned home, but decided against it. I had said my good-byes to the dead. It was time to get on with the business of living.

The general became the first elected president of Texas and moved the capital from the little town of Columbia, Texas, to the new town of Houston on Buffalo Bayou named in his honor. On the first anniversary of the Battle of San Jacinto, the now President Houston held a grand celebration in the new capital. I actually got an invitation from the general himself. Luke, Rachel, and Ma agreed to come with me to help with Danielle. A grand ball was held in the newly erected capital building which was attended by all the government officials and important people in Houston. I brought Danielle with me, of course, so the General could meet her, but decided to leave her with Ma while Luke, Rachel, and I attended the ball. I wasn't even sure if I would get to speak with the general, but was I in for a surprise. Luke, Rachel, and I bought formal dress clothes for the occasion when we arrived in Houston, and so felt that we at least blended in with all those supposedly important people. At least we thought we did. No one spoke to us at the ball and we were beginning to feel a little uncomfortable.

Luke had just taken Rachel out on the dance floor for a waltz, when I heard a familiar voice say, "Mrs. Autry, would you like to dance?" It was the general himself smiling that boyish grin that had always belied the seriousness in his blue eyes. He had never smiled much during the war, and it was nice to see him smiling now. We danced and danced and caught up on the events in each other's lives.

I told him about my family moving to Texas, and about Danielle. Suddenly he stopped dancing and gave me a stern look, "Do you mean to tell me that you were pregnant at San Jacinto?" I slowly nodded as he shook his head. "If something would have happened to you and that baby—"

"It would have been my fault," I finished. "Besides, I didn't know I was pregnant at the time and nothing happened."

He continued to give me a stern look for a moment longer, than began to smile a little smugly. "I wish you would have brought the little tike with you. Why didn't you bring her along?"

"Well, sir," I began hesitantly, "I did bring her to Houston, but she is five months old and is very strong-willed and rambunctious. I was afraid she might make a scene at the ball tonight, so I left her at the hotel with my mother. I thought I would bring her and Ma by your office tomorrow so that you can meet them both."

"So...like mother, like daughter," he replied, laughing. "Good."

I just rolled my eyes at him and grinned. We danced a few more dances and I could tell by the envious looks I was getting from several ladies that the general probably wouldn't remain a bachelor for long. It was great to see him again.

While we were there, President Houston—it is so hard not to call him General—introduced me to one of the leading citizens in Houston, James Turner, who owned a ranch outside of town. I also danced with Mr. Turner and really didn't think any more about him after going back home, until he came to Gonzales to buy some cattle. In fact, he came to Gonzales several times to buy cattle and always managed to call on me at the house during these visits. I really liked Mr. Turner. He was a good, moral man, and the fact that he was handsome and wealthy definitely added to his appeal. We married in June of 1842, and Danielle and I moved to Houston after selling my land in Gonzales to Luke. I felt very sad about selling the place, but I knew that part of my life was over now and I needed to let it go. James and I had a very good marriage. He also disapproved of slavery and paid every man who worked for him a fair wage. I opened a small school to teach the children of our workers, since, unfortunately, more and more slave owners were moving into the Republic who didn't believe black or working class white children should have an education. We had two sons, James Jr. and John. Although they would be forced to endure the horrors of Civil War, they would both go on to become very successful young men.

The next time I saw the general was February 19, 1846, in the new capital of Austin, Texas. This was the day Texas officially joined the United States. Texas's period as a country had proven to be a very tumultuous, often difficult one. We never had any money in the treasury, Mexico continually threatened to invade, and we also had problems with the Indians. The general served as president twice and had always wanted the United States to annex Texas. He asked me to stand by him for the ceremony of lowering the Texas flag and raising the United States flag. I knew that Texas annexation was for the best, but for some reason it filled me with sadness. I thought of all the people who had fought so hard for Texas independence and now it seemed she was losing that independence. Then President Anson Jones made a speech which he ended by saying, "The final act in this great drama is now performed. The Republic of Texas is no more." Tears filled my eyes as he lowered the Lone Star flag and handed it to the general.

The last time I saw the general was in 1863. That was a very bad time for my family and for the country. I was fifty-one years old and the country had descended into a Civil War between the North and the South over the issue of slavery. There was definitely nothing civil about it. In fact, the country was a bloody mess!

James, Jr. and John were off fighting for the South with General Lee. Even though I disagreed with slavery, I understood they felt they had no choice but to fight for their home. Danielle's husband was also off fighting with Lee, and she was living with James and me until he hopefully returned home. The general was seventy years old, and his son, Sam Jr., was also fighting in the war. The general had been forced to resign as governor of Texas because he wouldn't take the oath of allegiance to the Confederacy. It had been a very sad time for the Houstons, especially the general because he so loved his Texas.

I had received a letter from his wife Margaret that the general was coming to Houston to visit the old battle ground and would I please meet him there. Margaret and the general had married in 1840, two years before James and I, and I had had the privilege of receiving letters from her from time to time since the general was always too busy to write. I had first met her at the annexation ceremony and had found her to be a very nice, pleasant person with whom I enjoyed visiting. I immediately wrote her back to let her know I would gladly meet with him.

I arrived early at the battlefield and set out a picnic lunch under our great oak tree where Santa Anna surrendered. The general and his servant Jeff arrived not long after. The general seemed to have aged so much since I had last seen him. His once tall, strong, commanding body was now bent with age, and I hurried over to his buggy to help him descend and walk over to the tree. Jeff joined us and we ate our lunch in silence listening to the seagulls crying overhead and the water lapping against the shore. Finally Jeff went back to give the horse some water and leave the general and me to talk.

I asked him if he had heard from Sam Jr. and he told me that Sam had been wounded and had returned home. I told him I had received letters from my boys and both for the time being were safe and sound.

After a little silence, I said, "General, sometimes I wish we could have remained our own country and then maybe we wouldn't be in this mess. Mainly I worry about my boys who feel as if they have to fight with Texas and the secessionists even though James has never owned slaves and has always paid his hands whatever their color." I paused for a moment gathering my thoughts. "When Texas was young, all of the people who first came here worked together and fought together. Except for the Indians with whom you had established a truce before the revolution began and the established Tejano families who had already settled here, we were all basically misfits, running away from something, running towards something, or just looking for something better. It didn't matter if you were white, black, or Tejano, we had a common goal: to begin a new life where everyone had the opportunity to own land, to succeed, and later to fight Santa Anna's tyranny."

"But lately it seems that a lot of outsiders have moved into Texas who don't understand or really identify with Texas or her origins. They just want a lot of land on which to grow cotton and get rich. So instead of remembering how we once all worked together, we are allowing ourselves to be dragged into the mud of slavery, prejudice, and war. Most Texans now distrust Tejanos because of Mexico's repeated threats to invade, and we have seceded from the Union and become a slave state. The whole thing just makes me sick."

The general just looked at me sadly and said, "I know, Samantha, I tried to keep Texas from seceding. I told them that they couldn't win the war because, even if God happened to be on our side, the North is determined to preserve the Union. President Lincoln actually offered to send me fifty thousand troops if I would fight to keep Texas in the Union. I refused because I knew I couldn't make the people remain in the Union willingly, no matter how much force I used. And they turned against me, Samantha! My fellow Texans, whom I have fought for and worked for and sacrificed for almost all of my adult life, turned against me! So I resigned as governor and now I can't help but worry about my Texas."

"I know, General. I'm afraid too. I'm afraid that the South will suffer greatly just as you predicted. I'm afraid my sons will die along with many more of their generation. And even after it is all over, I'm afraid that the country may never recover from the hard feelings and resentments that this war will cause. We may never truly be united ever again!"

Then, despite the fear gnawing at the pit of my stomach, I felt my heart go out to the general because he looked so tired, beaten, and sad. "Don't worry, General, Texas has been through tough times before, and although I think she will pay a heavy price this time, I believe, God willing, she will find her way again. I believe all the people of Texas will once again come together because we will realize we need each other. We will remember that we are more than our race, more than our cultures. We will remember that we are Texans, and we stand tall when we stand together, strong, resilient, defeating tyranny and achieving great things."

We talked a while longer about the battle and the people who had fought alongside of us: Juan, Hendrick, Deaf Smith, Colonel Crockett, Colonel Bowie, and Colonel Travis. We shared any information either of us knew about the ones still living and shared remembrances about those who had died. Finally I noticed the sun beginning to sink toward the west, and I knew the general and Jeff had a ways to go to get home. Also, I could tell the general was getting tired. I motioned to Jeff to come over.

"Sir," Jeff said, "I think we should start heading home."

"Yes, Jeff, I believe we should."

Jeff and I helped the general to his feet, and I gave him a great big hug. "I enjoyed our visit, General. You take care of yourself."

He hugged me for a long while and said, "When you get my age, you hate saying good-bye."

"Then let's don't," I said. "We'll see each other again. For now we're just going home."

"Yes, you're right, my little spy," said the general as we walked back to his buggy. "It's time to go home."

REFERENCES

Tinkle, Lon. *The Alamo*. 5th Ed. New York, New York: McGraw Hill Book Company, 1958.

Hardin, Stephen. *Texian Iliad*. Austin, Texas: University of Texas Press, 1996.

Haley, James. *Sam Houston*. Norman, Oklahoma: University of Oklahoma Press, 2002.

Groneman, William. *David Crockett Hero of the Common Man*. New York, New York: Tom Doherty Associates, LLC, 2005.

Wallis, Michael. *David Crockett The Lion of the West*. New York, New York: W. W. Norton And Company, Inc. 2011.

De la Pena, Jose Enrique. Translated by Carmen Perry. *With Santa Anna in Texas*. College Station, Texas: Texas A&M University Press, 1997.

Scheina, Robert L. *Santa Anna: A Curse Upon Mexico*. Dulles, Virginia: Brassey's Inc., 2002.

Barr, Alwynn. *The African Texans*. College Station, Texas: Texas A&M University Press, 2004

Ross, John. "Black Texans Fought for Texas Independence." *Cherokeean Herald*, February 28, 2007.

Jackson, Ron. "In the Alamo's Shadow." *True West Magazine.* February, 1998.

Dr. Juliet Walker. "Free Blacks." Black History in Texas. March 15, 2003. www.utexas.edu/world/texasblack history/ FreeBlacks.html.

Margaret Swett Henson, "Anglo-American Colonization," *Handbook of Texas Online.*

Douglas Hale. "Free Blacks." *Handbook of Texas Online.*

Troop Movements Map of the Texian Revolution-Obtained from the San Jacinto Monument Museum.

The Alamo. John Lee Hancock, dir. Perf. Dennis Quaid, Billy Bob Thorton, Jason Patric. Touchstone Pictures, 2004.